The Last Summer of Reason

Tahar Djaout

TRANSLATED FROM THE FRENCH BY

Marjolijn de Jager

FOREWORD BY

Wole Soyinka

INTRODUCTION TO THE BISON BOOKS EDITION BY

Alek Baylee Toumi

University of Nebraska Press
Lincoln and London

Originally published as *Le Dernier été de la raison*,
© 1999 Éditions du Seuil

English translation © 2001 by Marjolijn de Jager
Introduction © 2007 by the Board of Regents of
the University of Nebraska
Foreword © 2001 by Wole Soyinka
Manufactured in the United States of America

First Nebraska paperback printing: 2007

Library of Congress Cataloging-in-Publication Data
Djaout, Tahar, 1954–
[Dernier été de la raison. English]
The last summer of reason / Tahar Djaout; translated from the
French by Marjolijn de Jager; foreword by Wole Soyinka;
introduction to the Bison Books edition by Alek Baylee Toumi.
p.   cm.
ISBN 978-0-8032-1591-7 (pbk.: alk. paper)
I. De Jager, Marjolijn.   II. Title.
PQ3989.2.D538D4713   2007
843'.914—dc22   2007012430

Introduction

Alek Baylee Toumi

In March 1993 three Algerian intellectuals, Hafid Sen-
hadri, Djillali Lyabes, and Laadi Flici, were assassinated
by Islamists. On May 17, 1993, Omar Belhouchet, editor in chief of the independent Francophone daily *El
Watan*, miraculously survived an assassination attempt.
On Wednesday, May 26, 1993, journalist Tahar Djaout
was shot in the parking lot of his apartment with two
bullets in the head. After eight days in a coma, Djaout
died on June 3, 1993, at the age of thirty-nine, leaving
behind a widow and three little girls.

From Paris, London, and Washington DC, "refugee"
Algerian Islamists, members of the Islamic Salvation
Front (FIS), claimed responsibility for many of these
murders. Algeria, a country that had seen all kinds of
tragedies during its millennia of history, was in a state
of shock. On December 29, 1993, Islamist militants
killed poet Youcef Sebti in Algiers by slitting his throat.
Without a doubt, new *Khmers verts* were eliminating all
those who dared to stand in their way.

The spring of 1993 marked the beginning of
the genocide of intellectuals in Algeria. It was a well-

planned intellectuocide, with lists of people to eliminate often posted in neighborhood mosques. In 1994 and 1995 there were more journalists murdered in Algeria than in the rest of the world as the country became the new killing fields. We should bear in mind that, like Salman Rushdie, Djaout and all these intellectuals were secular or mainstream Muslims, moderate and tolerant; that they all represented intelligence and dissent; and that their executioners, the terrorists, are called *Islamists*. As we should not confuse victims with assassins, it is important not to confuse Muslims with Islamists and blame Muslim victims for crimes committed by Islamists. As Rushdie once said, the majority of victims killed by Islamists are Muslims. Indeed, Muslims remain the West's strongest allies and its best hope in its war against Islamist terrorism.

THE ALGERIAN CIVIL WAR

In 1947 Albert Camus finished his novel *The Plague* with the following sentence:

> He [Rieux] knew what those jubilant crowds did not know but could have learned from books; that the plague bacillus never dies or disappears for good; that it can lie dormant for years and years in furniture and linen-chests; that it bides its time in bedrooms, cellars, trunks, and bookshelves; and that perhaps the day would come when, for the bane and the enlightening of men, it would rouse up its rats again, and send them forth to die in a happy city."

Not long ago Algiers was a happy city, but in the early nineties it was invaded by the bacillus of a green plague. Algeria found itself in the midst of a bloody civil war, torn between the military-backed National Liberation Front (FLN) and the Islamist FIS. It was in this context of terror that Tahar Djaout founded his weekly newspaper *Ruptures* in January 1993.

I did not personally meet Djaout during my last stay in Algiers in the eighties, but I knew him through several mutual friends. I knew him through his novels *The Watchers* and *The Bone Seekers* and through the writings of his friend Rachid Mimouni, another persecuted Francophone novelist. Many of my friends, such as Akli, a classmate from Les Pères-Blancs, a French Catholic boarding school in Algiers, knew Djaout very well. During a trip to Montreal in December 1995, I saw Akli again in one of those cafés of exile, surrounded by many refugees. Akli would sometimes talk about Tahar Djaout with a lot of nostalgia and sadness. He used to say that Djaout "was a nice guy, a good man, who liked to laugh. . . . We used to have a beer together. . . . We did not think they would. . . . No, we did not think they would dare kill intellectuals." Then he would suddenly become silent, his eyes looking far off, drowned in the glacial Quebec winter. Akli used to be a journalist with Djaout at *Algérie Actualités*, Algeria's main weekly during the eighties.

In the footsteps of Kateb Yacine, perhaps the most important Francophone writer from North Africa,

Tahar Djaout will remain the novelist and the poet *engagé*, the upright reporter, and the incorruptible intellectual. In his "Letter from the Editor," published in the first issue of *Ruptures* in January 1993, Djaout wrote, "We will refuse Manichaeism and all blackmails that have a tendency to lock us up into logics of this type: 'it will be me or the one across who is worse than me,' 'if you're not with me you're against me.'" Djaout publicly rejected blackmails from Baathists—Stalinists of the FLN party—and from their former Islamist allies. At the risk of his life, he made the choice to stand up to both of them, which turned him into their privileged target.

Like an orphan whose father prematurely dies before the child's birth, Djaout's last novel did not have a name. The title is the first sentence of the fourth part of the book: "Boualem Yekker calls this season the last summer of reason." It is one of those summers of 1990 to 1992, reminiscent of the fiction *Fahrenheit 451*, when vigilante Islamists are burning French books, harassing intellectuals, and beating up unveiled women in the streets. The main character, a bookstore owner named Boualem, is threatened by the new inquisition.

As a young teenager in Algiers, I loved to go downtown to browse the many bookstores, especially the Librairie des Beaux-Arts. It was located in the heart of rue Didouche (formerly rue Michelet) not far from the School of Fine Arts and was run by a *pied-noir*—a French Algerian named Joaquim Grau, alias "Vincent."

It was in this bookstore that I bought many novels, poetry books, and my first record, *Le Jardin des Enfants* by
George Moustaki. Just like the narrator Boualem, Vincent had chosen to remain in Algiers despite the permanent threats. Alas, he was assassinated on February
21, 1994, inside his Librairie des Beaux-Arts. That year,
defenseless civilians were slaughtered by the hundreds
by the Islamic Armed Group (GIA). On Christmas Eve
1994 the GIA hijacked an Air France airbus flying from
Algiers to Paris, intending to crash it into the Eiffel
Tower. Fortunately, this tragic rehearsal of September
11 was aborted in Marseille as the plane was stormed
by French commandos when it stopped for refueling.

Brainwashed while attending the Algerian school,
Boualem Yekker's son and daughter become fundamentalists—born-again Islamists. Members of an obscure sect similar to the Moonies, they convert their
mother. Then the three of them desert the infidel father, a heretic Muslim who refuses to join their flock
of hate. It was not by accident that Djaout named his
main character Yekker. In Kabyle, the language of
the Berbers of Kabylie, where Djaout was from, *Yekker*
means "he stood up." "Ekker Amis Umazigh" (Stand
Up Son of the Free Man) was one of the first antico-
lonialist songs during the forties. A free man and a
poet himself, Djaout probably knew this chant of par-
tisans. In the novel Boualem Yekker is an ordinary citizen who peacefully resists the wild horde of Orwellian
big brothers, who watch relentlessly. They search gar-

bage for corks—the irrefutable proof of wine drinking, which will condemn a man to death. These children of hate draw up lists of infidels to be killed and have taken up the mission to eliminate all those who refuse to think like them or to follow them.

In Algeria there were two types of heretics on top of the lists of condemned people: *femminists* (pronounced "famminists") and journalists. Feminists, or womanists, represent those unveiled Muslim women, students, intellectuals, or working women who refuse to become second class citizens or subjects, euphemisms for *slave*. They refuse to become objects of shame, hidden in ambulatory jails called *hidjab* or *burka*; they ask to be treated as full citizens! Their demands have nothing to do with American feminism with its women's lib, its ERA, and its abortion rights. All they want are basic human rights, such as working outside the home to feed their family. They want to be able to dress normally, as an ordinary western woman would dress, to have the right to keep their salary, and the right to adoption. The second group, the journalists, are those Francophone children of Descartes, raised in method and doubt and who have the audacity to criticize. They dare to question everything when the whole truth that can exist is, according to Islamists, found in the Koran. Indeed, there is no room for doubt or dissent with fundamentalists; any criticism is often silenced with a silencer.

WHY DID THEY KILL INTELLECTUALS?

In 1989, with the advent of democracy, the new multi-party system, and the liberalization of the media, more than a dozen newspapers were born. In 1993 Tahar Djaout and a few friends founded *Ruptures*, a weekly dedicated to breaking with Islamo-Baathist ideology. One reason often given for Djaout's death is that he wrote in French, the language of colonization, and not in Arabic. This argument seems valid if one supposes there are only two languages in Algeria. However, this is a false assumption because there are not two but four languages in Algeria. There are two native languages, spoken by the majority of the people: Algerian Creole, a mixture of "French-Arabic-Berber" (or *farabic*), and Berber, such as Kabyle. There are also two written languages: French and classical Arabic, called *fusha*. French still remains the language of economic exchanges and intellectual production. Djaout could not have written in Kabyle (his native language) or in Algerian Creole. The former language had been a victim of cultural genocide while the latter has no alphabet. In order to write, Algerians must do so in French, a foreign language, or in classical Arabic, also a foreign language as *fusha* is not their native tongue. Djaout could have realistically only written *Ruptures* in French since the overwhelming majority of intellectuals in Algeria are Francophone.

Before his exile in 1994, novelist Rachid Mimouni

explained that all things that could be openings to modernity and the outside world—especially those people called *Francophones*, demonized by Islamo-Baathists accusing them of being the "Party of France"—became the privileged target of the inquisitors. After the assassination of Djaout, Arabic writer Tahar Ouattar made his infamous comment: "The death of Djaout is a loss for his family, a loss for France, but not for Algeria." Ouattar seemed to justify Djaout's death, killing him a second time with this cheap shot declaration. It is strange that these Taliban inquisitors never considered themselves the "Party of the Saudis," their main sponsors, or the "Party of Iran."

Many scholars have claimed that the Algerian civil war, with its two hundred thousand civilian victims, would not have happened had the military let Islamists take power in 1991 after the FIS won the parliamentary elections. This is another false statement as the FIS won the first round of elections *with fraud*. First, the FLN organizers splintered the democratic opposition into fifty parties and legalized the FIS in 1989, saying, "It is us or them." Then, 50 percent of the population did not vote at all because, since independence, they had been trained to vote yes or no for the sole candidate of the single party FLN in fixed elections. Many of those who voted for the FIS voted against the FLN to "throw the bums out." Moreover, western media have surprisingly forgotten to report that the FLN allowed Islamists to vote three, five, seven times, for their mother, wife, sisters, daughters, and any female in their family. These elections should thus have been called null and void because a democratic election means one person, one vote. With all the terror and cheating, the Islamists received less than 25 percent of the vote, meaning that 75 percent of the population did not vote for them. Let's also remember that Adolf Hitler was democratically elected in Germany in a similar climate of terror.

SCHOOL: AT THE HEART OF THE PROBLEM

In his "Letter from the Editor" in *Ruptures* of January 1993, Djaout wrote, "Among the structures to be remodeled as fast as possible is the educational system. It is useless to repress fundamentalism if the Algerian school continues to prepare for us new packs of fundamentalists who, in their turn, will take up arms in ten or fifteen years."

Djaout and many observers point the finger at the school system, victim of the politics of Arabization. Formerly secular and French-speaking, the Algerian school did not become secular and Arabic-speaking but rather Islamist. How come? After independence Algerian president Ahmed Ben Bella claimed three times, "We are Arabs," even though the majority of the population was not of Arab descent. In order to Arabize the schools, Ben Bella asked for help from his friend Gamal Abdel Nasser, then president of Egypt.

Nasser sent some Arabic professors to Algeria, but he also sent unemployed Egyptians without any teaching credentials. And he also threw in members of the Islamic Brotherhood, who went to Algeria to convert opportunists and religious zealots to their sect. This is a sad truth that many do not like to talk about as it is rather disturbing.

With time, the Algerian school was no longer open to the outside world and its dispensing of modern teaching. Placed in the hands of Baathists, Islamist preachers, and reactionary men, it became a school of hate. After one generation the Algerian school looked like one of those Afghan *madrasas*, creating ignorant Taliban fanatics. Instead of citizens, the school has been mostly producing high school drop-outs and poorly prepared students—future soldiers of God. The wrecked school has become the Oran of Camus, with the plague in its courtyard. Inside, fundamentalist beasts pollute children's minds with racist and anti-Semitic propaganda and send them out to persecute their own family members.

The Last Summer of Reason takes place precisely in an Algiers of the inquisition, surrounded by Islamists in Afghan uniforms, bearded men in *kamis* robes, and women in dark *hidjabs*. But where did the Algiers of yesteryear go, the sunny city called *Alger la blanche* that the Romans named Icosium? If you have never visited Algiers, it is a big city of many millions of people, built on a hill, a city open to the Mediterranean. Algiers used to be a living city, a joyful city splashing with light, a laughing city with cafés, bars, and French bakeries at every street corner, similar to old quarters of Marseille or San Francisco, rushing down toward the sea. Algiers was the home of Camus, forced too into exile by French extreme right-wingers in 1940.

For millennia a crossroads between East and West, between Europe, Africa, and the Orient, Algeria has provided humanity with some of its greatest intellectuals. Whether in Latin, Arabic, or French, these intellectuals have always produced their writings in the language of the last colonizer. Alas, they have often ended up humiliated, excluded, persecuted, banned, exiled, or condemned to capital punishment. From Saint Augustine (born in Thagaste, nowadays Souk-Ahras), author of *The Confessions*, to Tahar Djaout, Albert Camus, Kateb Yacine, and Jacques Derrida, Algeria seems to punish its own intellectuals as would a cruel stepmother do with her stepchildren. Saint Augustine had problems with Donatists of the Roman era, Camus was excluded then condemned to death in 1956 by French ultra-colonialists, and Vichy France kicked Derrida out of Algiers's high school. After independence Kateb Yacine was censured then persecuted by FLN zealots, who released on him their Islamist *tonton macoutes*. Isn't it peculiar to see a country that gave birth to so many great minds eventually turn against them and abandon them to the hands of intolerance?

I do not know why, but Djaout's writings remind me of Pastor Martin Niemöller's famous poem:

> First they came for the Jews, and I did not speak out—because I was not a Jew.
> Then they came for the communists, and I did not speak out—because I was not a communist.
> Then they came for the trade unionist, and I did not speak out—because I was not a trade unionist.
> Then they came for me, and there was no one left to speak out for me."

Perhaps it is because both Niemöller and Djaout were persecuted by intolerance—one was a victim of Nazis and the other of Nazislamists. Both of them have left this life as little angels on a cloud, up in the heavens with other innocent victims of exclusion and hatred. I have often wondered if Djaout, lover of fine poetry as he was, knew this verse. One of his last writings seems to reply to it:

> Silence is death,
> and you, if you talk, you die,
> and if you remain silent, you die.
> So, speak out and die.

Djaout took a courageous stand. He spoke out perhaps a little too well and a little too loud, and he paid for it with his own life. His *engagement* and his intellectual integrity were unshakable. In the first issue of *Ruptures*, in his article "Hatred in Front of Us," echoing Germany's president, Djaout wrote, "If fascism triumphed in Germany at the end of the 30s, it is not because there were a lot of fascists, but because there were not enough democrats." And if there are not enough democrats today, people to stand up for liberty and justice, to denounce fascists and fascislamists, to oppose their totalitarian projects and their murderous hates and support Muslims like Djaout and Rushdie, then for our own calamity the plague will rouse up its rats again and send them forth to die in our happy cities.

Table of Contents

Tahar Djaout was assasinated in the spring of 1993. The unedited manuscript for this book was found among his papers after his death. The work was published in French without alteration, other than to correct some minor inconsistencies.

Foreword
A Voice that Would Not Be Silenced

This voice from the grave urges itself on our hearing. For let no one be in any doubt—the life-and-death discourse of the twenty-first century is unambiguously the discourse of fanaticism and intolerance. We can subsume this however we will under other concerns—economy, globalization, hegemonism, the arms race, AIDS, even environmental challenges; some of these rightly dominate the attention of the world. Ultimately, however, we come face to face with one overweening actuality: the proliferation of a mind-set that feeds on a compulsion to destroy other beings who do not share, not even the same beliefs, but specific subcategories of such beliefs. It is a mind-set that destroys the creative or adventurous of any community. It continues to prove efficient at fueling devastating conflicts all over the world, often in places that are remote from the accustomed circuits of global attention.

Attempts are made throughout history to plumb the depths of this singular mind-set, one that appears to find fertile ground most readily in ideology and religion. The findings of such inquiries—and have we not all, at some time or the other, encountered walking repositories of such convictions?—can be frightening. For we soon come to a realization that such minds are unreachable, permanently in the dark ages, in the darkest ages of superstition, the home of phantoms, of a terror of the unknown, the phobia for every new or alien experience, a phobia of such all-consuming intensity that, for survival, it must eliminate all doubters. It is the setting of the mind, not on questions, but on the mantra "I am right, you are wrong," whose ultimate goal of unreason is "I am right; you are dead!"

But is it all about ideology or religion? Or has it to do just as much with power and domination? Conformism is an elementary conditioning of society that is essential for the exercise of power, be the route one of the imposition of a secular or a theocratic ideology. The history of censorship is an old one, censorship not merely of the written word, but of the spoken, censorship in dress codes, human relationships, dietary choices, lifestyles, and even thought. The culture of the taboo appears to have evolved with the earliest human cohabitation, its origins—often traceable to strategies for combating shortages and ensuring communal survival—now dissipated in the mists of antiquity. What remains of the taboo is its opportunistic mechanism of control—that is, the enthronement of the monopoly of power—by a class, usually a religious elite, through mystification. No matter how elaborate the scriptures that now sanctify the original taboos, or the veneration that time has accorded such scriptures, they remain nothing but jealously guarded mechanisms of power by a few over the many. What once translated as "taste not of the fruits of this tree" has not changed in character. The fruits of the forbidden tree remain knowledge and inquiry—ironically, the original authors of the fable of the Garden of Eden were far more honest than their successors and heirs.

We know that no one is born with such mind closure; it must be carefully inseminated and nurtured, often with a single-minded ruthlessness. But why, in the past century, has this tendency appeared to have gained in such murdeous intensity? Are we confronted here perhaps with a parallel phenomenon of the deliberate cultivation of unawareness, an attitude of hoping, silently, that the menace will eat itself up, collapse inwards from its own untenable doctrines, that it will vanish if it is simply ignored? The strategy of evasion sometimes involves attributing far-reaching causes to this phenomenon, thus becoming a willing tool in the accommodation of the culture of intolerance. An example: highlighting the slights of history that have been inflicted by external forces, accompanied usually by imposition of hostile values and alien customs. History is thus used to justify both a hostility to and a rejection of new ideas, conveniently dubbed alien. Following, as a matter of course, is the internal repression of those who are themselves part of the terrain of external aggression, but refuse to remain eternal prisoners of the resented history. Indeed, the latter are considered far more potent enemies than the external agents of that history. They are traitors from within, who must be forcibly weaned from their delusions or simply eliminated. We are thus faced with a category of permanent victims, victims of the murderous arrogance of their own kind, victims of a messianic zeal that parades itself as divine consciousness for the redress of history. At the forefront of such victims are the creative minds, the writers, artists and visionaries of society.

Conveniently designated purveyors of alien values, they become disposable. Never mind the fact
that they quarry inwards into their own society and
culture, query its own internal contradictions, and
attempt to highlight antecedent cultural values that
have become dislodged from popular consciousness
by the obscurantism of the new gospelers. Have they
dared propose a preexistent right of women to dig-
nity, insist on their place as equal members of the
human race? Or simply observed that conformism is
actually a retrogressive face of evolution, and that
the authentic life instinct is toward originality and
variety? What matters is that they are identified
as subversives who reveal alternatives to a sim-
plistic understanding and ordering of society. If writers, they possess an armory of unholy words with
which to rephrase or reinterpret, for the purposes
of demystification, even passages from those same
scriptures that seemingly encrypt the doctrine of
conformism or female subservience. They embrace a
morality that compels them to challenge the authority of the fatal interpreter of the divine word. But it is
not the writers alone who find themselves gravely at
risk. Other clerics whose reading of the holy book
lacks the desired homicidal zeal are equally marked

for elimination. And then, of course, the suspected carriers of this new contamination, the consumers.

It is thus essential that we take note that Tahar Djaout bears witness from within his own society, from within his own milieu, and in defense of his assailed humanity. But let no one be tempted to narrow the bane of bigotry and intolerance to just one milieu from which this powerful testimony has emerged. Lucid and poignant, it is an exploration of the very phenomenon of intolerance, and its application is universal, as in the best allegories that are grounded in reality. At the same time, however, we dare not take refuge in universalisms when the victims are specific and immediate. It is not a universal principle that gets stabbed, shot, and even mutilated. It is a very specific voice, one that has made a conscious choice and died in defense of that choice. And it is only by recognizing that individuality that we are enabled to recollect, and respond to the fate of other individuals, to the fate of hundreds like Djaout, and the fate of hundreds of thousands on behalf of whom that voice has been raised, against whom the hand of atavism is also constantly raised, aiming ever more boldly for a body count that will pave the way of killers to a paradise of their imagining.

The most ambitious enemies of humanity are the absolutist interpreters of the Divine Will, be they Sikhs, Hindus, Jews, Christians, Muslims, born-agains of every religious calling. In the United States, after nearly three years on the run, a self-appointed "sword of God," raised against the upholders of the right to abortion, was finally arrested. From arson attacks on abortion clinics, he had graduated to righteous executions of doctors in their homes. His coreligionists openly cheered him, several protected him. Let such examples serve to remind us that the phenomenon of fanaticism is not always contingent on environment and history but is a teaching, nurturing, indoctrinating occupation. That certain social conditions provide congenial breeding grounds for susceptible human material is not in dispute, especially when the indoctrinating process can be linked, as already remarked, to real or imagined social or historical injustices. Nonetheless, the fanatic, intolerant mind, to be effectively countered, must first be addressed as a willfully manipulated, proliferating phenomenon. It is a contagion like any other known transmissible disease. The accommodative language of "political correctness," so fashionable in some of the world's largest democracies, must be recognized as a language of complicity with the league of darkness and intolerance in the life-and-death struggle of enlightenment and creativity. It comforts the proponents of terror and dehumanizes the victims even further, for it subsumes their trauma under a doctrine of relativity that denigrates their fundamental and universal right to life and freedom. The arrogant elimination of the Djaouts of our world must nerve us to pursue our own combative doctrine, namely: that peaceful cohabitation on this planet demands that while the upholders of any creed are free to adopt their own existential absolutes, the right of others to do the same is thereby rendered implicit and sacrosant. Thus the creed of inquiry, of knowledge and exchange of ideas, must be upheld as an absolute, as ancient and eternal as any other.

This posthumous allegory bequeathed to the world by Tahar Djaout is a literary gem that gleams from beyond the grave. It is also, surely, a humanistic testament, beamed at the complacent conscience of the world.

Wole Soyinka

The Last Summer of Reason

Sermon 1

The Omniscient Eye can light up at any moment to take your confusions and your little schemes by surprise or to tear you away from your shameful conspiracies. It puts you back in the vast circle of its brightness where you rediscover the annihilating evidence of your wretchedness. You then become a rabbit again, trembling with anxiety, driven into a corner when confronted by the thundering roar of conviction. You are unceremoniously pried away from the illusory universe your fantasies have set up and furnished. The Truth dissolves over you like an implacable bird of prey; it floods you, illuminates you, and pierces you with its rays. You feel transparent, prostrated, and tethered. And yet, delivered at the same time. You have been torn away from incongruous questioning, from the doubts plaguing your nights, from the anxieties tying your innards into knots. A benevolent but firm hand has put you back in the warm and protective lap of evidence. Like an umbilical cord, the halo that illuminates and guides the theories of your peers connects you to the mother-truth and to the immense and blessed humanity grace has chosen.

You cease to be alone. Forever. You have been taken in charge both in the here and now and in the world that is to follow. You are comfortably seated in the heart of the brotherhood of the blessed, which no heavenly gift will spurn: a limpid life untroubled by any inappropriate question, a sojourn of pure bliss in what prolongs this life.

Gone is disperion, gone are the byroads! All things will come back to their essence. Of what use are books when the Book exists to sate every curiosity and slake every thirst? Of what use are anxieties and painful questioning when inexhaustible serenity is within the heart's grasp?

At last the world has reached the equilibrium it should have had all along, were it not for the seditious philosophies and the devious interrogations that led the spirit of humanity astray by hauling it away from the paths of humility and salutary submission. Pride has finally been conquered! Time, the avenger, has ended up by coming and blowing down like a house of cards the structures built on insolent lies.

The Omniscient Eye can light up at any moment. It is blinding in its brilliance and at the same time in the truth it sheds. It is illuminating and confusing. Its prominence is like a millstone crushing half-light and hesitation. It is a forthright desire like a sword slashing into living flesh. For the halo of truth admits no shadow zone at all in which sin, doubt, or shameful reactions can still find any refuge.

The old field of humanity, choked up with unwanted plants, where bad shoots and perverse fruit were proliferating, had to be weeded and hoed. In the imperative and fervor of the action, blood was inevitably shed, the dew indispensable to the thirst of the world rising in the fire of redemption. Sometimes the double-edged sword is a blessed tool, the simple continuation of the well-guided hand inspired and moved by a superior order. Everything amounts to not recoiling, not knowing hesitation. For the least little inch of territory yielded can make room for the pernicious tree that, once again, will offer its fruits to humanity for the most irreparable of its misfortunes.

The blow was dealt to the root, so that the tree would not even take, so that its unnatural head would not emerge from the soil. Fortunately, the arm faced with salutary action did not falter, was neither stopped nor deviated by an inopportune sense of pity. This is how they have always acted, those who in the night of sacrilege opened the dazzling path of faith. What would they have conveyed to us had their desire flagged? We are their worthy heirs, the upholders of their faith. Like them, uncompromisingly and with conviction, we have sliced into the foul flesh of agnosticism. Glory to the discerning forces that shouldered us, galvanized us, and brought us together in victory!

The Eye can intervene at any moment with its disdainful magnanimity. You are then like the puppy terrorized by the sight or scent of a wild beast. You huddle, tail between your legs, submissive, sides trembling in agitation. Your pitiful secrets are forced out into the open like the bundles of a vagabond, your misery is dragged out under the sun, stabbed by haughty stares. You would have given anything if only tomorrow would never come with its procession of verdicts, if only all life would be terminated, instantly struck down by lightning. For to you the future has the face of squalid shame. You beg for annihilation, for the benevolence of an unbending arm that flings you into an abyss of peace. You loudly shout for the just wrath that will destroy you.

People must be forged by the use of the absolute. And, to that effect, they must be taken in early childhood. Erase doubt from their hearts and questions from their heads. The Great Work comes at this price, the price of indefatigable effort that takes up every day and every night.

Nevertheless, we have succeeded. Glory to Him who guides us in the desert without worldly reference points, who reaffirms us in our hour of doubt, and who enlightens us in the face of adversity's darkness. The sight of His face—His face that knows no artifice—brings the day of immutable decisions at this price. We shall forever be the inhabitants of His benevolence.

Tighten your ranks, people whom grace has visited, so that no depraved person can slip in between you and be the bearer of the seed of destructive questioning once more. Fuel your vigilance so that the gentle but dreadful inferno of faith remains brightly lit! We shall not always be there to watch over your consciences. One day the Eye may vanish.

The Vigilant Brothers

The road curves or runs straight depending on the line cut into the rock. Rumbling of the raging sea. The waves pounce on the parapets and then explode into foam, of which some ragged beads land on the road, which is completely clear. A few cars shoot past along the rectilinear stretches.

From time to time, a monstrous green motorcycle with heavy cylinders catches up with a car, keeping pace with it. With requisite helmet and beard, a Vigilant Brother scrutinizes the suspicious vehicle. He inspects the interior. If by chance there is a couple inside, there is a strong possibility that the V.B. will ask the driver to move to the right and stop in the parking strip so that he can check the identity papers to verify the passengers' conjugal or family relationship. The scrutiny also does its utmost to detect a bottle of alcohol or any other forbidden product. These V.B.s act as if they are in a new kind of western in which they play at collecting as many scalps of heathens and offenders of the laws of God as possible.

Road signs form a regular parade: *No one is above the Faith. God exterminates usurers. Woe to a people who let things be run by a woman. He will annihilate our enemies. If you are sick, He alone can heal you.*

Heavy rain begins to fall. Boualem Yekker speeds up to escape from a disaster. One or two hours of rain like this will be enough to make the streets impassable; the city suffers from a thorny problem with its gutters that it seems not to want (or be able?) to resolve. Boualem is thinking of an anecdote he read in his English book more than thirty years ago but which he still remembers. On a stormy day someone is visiting an Irishman; the rain is pouring through the dilapidated roof. "Why don't you repair your roof?" the visitor asks. "In this weather?" the Irishman answers. "You must be mad!" The person pays him a second visit, in the summer this time, and remembering the decaying roof, he suggests that his host repair it. "What for?" the Irishman replies. "It's not raining."

In situations that are growing more and more frequent, Boualem Yekker makes himself forget the present and calls upon memories and images. He lets himself be guided by words, veritable life preservers, which carefully bring him to familiar shores. He likes being glued to certain images that hold him as a willing prisoner far from a gruesome-faced present.

Boualem clings ferociously to these images as if he feels the day will come when no evasion, not even through the imagination, will be allowed any longer. Yes, he often has the impression that the days of dreaming are numbered. Boualem takes great care to resuscitate as many distant and incomplete faces and landscapes as possible before it is too late and there is no way out of the chaos. He crisscrosses these images in every direction, torn between the desire to drink from them greedily and the desire to control them for fear of exhausting his reserve too quickly.

These moments of reverie are refreshing mirages sweetening the world's inexorable drought. Life has ceased to be inflected in the present. Boualem is one of the people suffering from a new malady: an over-developed memory. Moreover, among this perse-cuted minority, memory very often goes into a panic for having been solicited and twisted: faces, places, and objects go adrift, fragments subjected to a dis-orderly game of emulsion or magnetization. Many elements cancel each other out, intersect or merge in a dizzying jumble. There comes a moment when, as you seek memory to take you out of the present, you encounter only a vague dream landscape in which the landmarks fall apart. A kind of night settles in where the shadows of memory grow restless. Sometimes they take on a sharper profile, as if they were passing in front of a light. In this whirlwind there are images of which the shock is unbearable; they shake you roughly, expel you from your dream, and, with your feet and hands tied, bring you back to merciless reality.

The rain passes quickly, even if the sky holds on to a bilious color. The road is flooded and the water sprays in violent spurts from beneath the tires. Even on this ribbon of tarmac the rain has awakened earthy and organic rural smells. In reality, they are exuded by a strip of land running along the road. A V.B. passes at high speed, the wheels of his motorcycle hurling a screeching spray of water.

Boualem Yekker associates the smells the rain brings with beauty. The beauty of people and things. Of sensations. The beauty of art, stretching us with overwhelming feelings, elevating us, and causing us to resonate. Fortunately, Boualem is neither elegant nor talented. This protects him from the V.B.s' attacks and violence. For, in the new era the country is living through, what is persecuted above all, and more than people's opinions, is their ability to create and propagate beauty. After the first public and dramatic trials brought against materialists, laypeople, and followers of all kinds of atheism, it did not take the inquisitors long to realize that the individuals they were judging were only a kind of offshoot, the effect and not the cause, and that the roots and the trunk of the evil lay elsewhere, able to go into greening again, burgeon once more to bring forth other unnatural fruits.

As long as music can transport the spirit, painting can make the core bloom with a rapture of colors, and poetry can make the heart pound with rebellion and hope, they will have gained nothing. To affirm their victory, they knew what they had to do. They broke musical instruments, burned rolls of film, slashed the canvases of paintings, reduced sculptures to rubble, and they were permeated with the exalted feeling that they were thereby pursuing and completing the purifying and grandiose work of their ancestors battling anthropomorphism. No terrestrial face should compete with His Face, no work of beauty created by a human hand should come close to His Beauty, no passion whatsoever should rival His resplendent Love.

As another V.B. passes by, Boualem suddenly feels small and vulnerable, almost pathetic. His secrets, his incongruity are exposed abruptly to the bright light of day. Bookseller. He does not create questions and beauty, but he does contribute to the dissemination of revolt and beauty. He, a modest woodcutter, does contribute to feeding the bonfire of ideas and improper dreams. He looks at himself in the rearview mirror to check his anguish. Yes, his decline is undeniable; it is quite visibly there: in his low and wrinkled forehead, in his inexpressive and tired eyes protected by horn-rimmed glasses. The face of a real clod. He cannot take the decoding of his disgrace any lower.

In this world advocating rigorism and submission to a higher order, Boualem is almost ashamed of selling speculations, dreams, and fantasies in the form of essays, novels, or adventure stories. The keepers of the new order apply themselves to making any citizen endowed with more than the humility and permissible banality of the standard citizen feel guilty. Those who have knowledge, talent, elegance, or physical beauty are reviled for their "privileges" and urged to make honorable amends in order to be integrated into the herd of submissive and blessed believers.

Confronted with the determination of the V.B.s, Boualem is comforted by one thing: the insignificance of his person, which his rearview mirror has just reconfirmed one more time. In this once so happy city, henceforth subject to the obliteration and ugliness asceticism requires, in this city transformed into a desert from which every oasis has disappeared, it is difficult for the keepers of the new order to see an enemy in Boualem Yekker. Is that not why they allow him to quietly continue his bookseller's activities?

When will the quake happen?

As the sun goes down, the shadow of the trees lengthen. Like a sagacious cat, the wind plays with papers and dead leaves, whirling them around where they are. Shadows pass: people have acquired a way of sneaking around instead of walking.

For more than a year now, Boualem Yekker has had the feeling he is living in an anonymous time and space, unreal and temporary, in which neither hours nor seasons nor places have the least characteristic of their own or the least importance. It is as if he were living a blank life, waiting for things to take on their weight, their colors, and their flavor again. It is as if the world had abandoned its appearance, its attributes, and its various functions, in disguise for as long as a carnival lasts.

What Boualem Yekker suffers from most of all is loneliness. Sometimes he is astonished to note how little our own life belongs to us, to what extent it becomes useless as soon as one is confronted with oneself, freed from the conflicts, bondage, worries, or joys those to whom our destiny is linked impose on or bring to us. There is an uncontrollable panic in finding oneself alone with the world.

Now that his wife and children have left him, his existence seems freer to him but also flat, and very much so, without any rough spots, without the unexpected and without meaning. It is a kind of frightening straight line, or rather a circular figure that turns around and around absurdly, without the resting point of a break or the perspective of a vanishing line.

He is beginning to get used to the banality of his life, but also, and above all, of his death. He could die any moment without disrupting or touching anyone. The only person to be sad perhaps would be Ali Elbouliga who, by losing him, would find himself deprived not of a beloved companion but of a reference point in the nebula of the everyday. Boualem Yekker's bookstore is a place where Ali Elbouliga spends a great deal of time, which does not in any way bother the bookseller, who, for months now, has had almost no customers at all. The two men spend hours conversing or being silent, while the beam of sunlight coming in through a corner of the window slowly moves around the shop until it disappears into the back room where books, too hazardous to be seen in the window or on the shelves inside, lie piled up.

Whatever the theme of the discussion, the great question haunting Ali Elbouliga inevitably arises sooner or later: when will the earthquake happen? Boualem can usually guess the moment the question is to be posed, for it is often preceded by a visible outer sign: Ali Elbouliga suddenly loses interest in the discussion. With his gaze distant and his mind absent, he nervously moves his lips while his whole body shakes. Then, having traveled through his body as it clears an arduous and painful path before reaching the harbor of his lips, the question finally erupts. When it is formulated, Ali Elbouliga enters a realm of great calm, like a sick person who has exhausted himself and is about to fall asleep. Obviously, he expects no answer; having articulated so crushing a question has depleted his energies and his curiosity.

Since the new order was established, Ali Elbouliga's visits have become much more frequent, for he, too, is a pariah: he doesn't say the five prayers and his neighbors avoid him with conspicuous contempt. But what discredits him most in the eyes of his entourage is his having formerly been a member of a popular-music orchestra in which he played the mandolin, that round-bellied instrument like a woman's belly calling to be caressed.

Aside from the commanding call of the muezzin, all music has now been banished from the city. All invisible and mysterious things that join forces to make life more beautiful and more stimulating have ceased delivering their lifeblood and murmuring their secrets. The world has become aphasic, opaque, and sullen; it is wearing mourning clothes. It has ceased existing, undoubtedly to punish those who have hurt it, who have called forth those lights and those scents that sometimes used to be so dazzling— especially at dusk—that you could only welcome them with sorrow, dazed, overcome, and losing your balance and your sense of measure beneath the weight of so generous a gift.

Now, while the wind is having a good time with papers and leaves outside, Boualem Yekker and Ali Elbouliga are in the semidarkness of the bookstore, like two pariahs or two plotters ill at ease in the light. They have already acquired the reflexes of a shadow tribe. Like night animals or the deep insides of cities, they will soon be able to move about and even to work without needing any light at all; they will be able to slip around the furniture without upsetting or turning anything over, without making the slightest noise. They will be able to slither, to flatten themselves, to unite with angles and corners. They will manage to make themselves invisible from the arrogant population, filled with certainties, prowling the streets and the daylight hours.

They stay side by side, without a word, as if being mute had become their new condition. As if their destiny, from now on, were to listen without responding to voices bearing a truth they proclaim in the streets, the stadiums, and the mosques. The country has entered an era in which questions are not asked, for questions are daughters of disquiet or arrogance, both fruits of temptation and the food of sacrilege.

Ali Elbouliga's enigmatic face is troubled by a nervous tic, his strange green eyes dilating in the half-light. Is he going to start talking again about the imminent upheaval? His thin cheeks are badly shaven; here and there short little tufts of hair have escaped the razor blade. Did he shave himself in the dark?

The earthquake is not what is bothering Elbouliga.

"It seems that spare tires are about to be banned. The new lawmakers interpret their presence in a car as an indication of the little faith we have in the Creator's ability to bring us to a safe haven. If He wants to leave us stranded in the middle of the road, it is because that is what He has decided to do and we only have to bow before His will.

"There are many other pieces of news, all equally puzzling. According to the rumors, there will soon be hospitals for men and hospitals for women. Any person caught outside a mosque at the hour of prayer will have to answer for his offense before a religious tribunal. Just a few types of clothing will be sold, and citizens will be obliged to wear them.

"That probably is a law concocted in complicity with some high-placed religious dignitary who also happens to be a textile magnate.

"That is how they spread rumors so they'll make their way into the consciousness of the citizens, thus preparing them for any extravagance, any excess."

A shadow approaches the bookstore, stops in front of the window, and looks at the few books displayed. It does sometimes happen that someone slows down or actually stops, looking at length at the illustrated jackets as if discovering the miracle of color for the first time; as if underneath the covers he surmises a world of dreams, brooks, trees, wild animals; a world in which tenderness, fantasy, and escape are permitted. But the curious rarely dare to come in. They are afraid to venture into this Aladdin's lair, into this appealing but suspect place, which they will perhaps not leave unscathed.

After first looking all around, the shadow that had paused in front of the bookstore disappears on tiptoe, suddenly aware that its reprehensible curiosity has perhaps been noticed.

Ali Elbouliga begins to tremble, a shivering that has nothing to do with the coolness of the dusk. A violent rush goes through him; he is under the impression that the earth's tremor he has so been dreading and expecting from one day to the next has changed his body into an epicenter. His memory opens up under the shock wave. The music submerges him, floods over him. The mandolin, the imprisoned soul of Ali's hands, has begun to resonate, to croon and sob. Lightheartedness (even if mixed with a touch of melancholy) was once the world's mistress, and notes would be born and rise fearlessly and without restraint. They would sing of fierce desire, of wandering beneath inclement skies, but also of the friend's dwelling where thirst is quenched and wounds are healed.

When had he learned to extract so much laughter, so many laments and avowals from the instrument? He cannot remember with any certainty. What he does remember much more clearly is the face that for him remains linked to his mandolin: the bony and lordly face of old Tayeb, looking like a distinguished ascetic. In his dark and cool hideaway in the heart of the old Casbah, he would make small objects out of wood, bone, and tortoiseshell. Did he manage to make his living off this crazy activity? Work and subsistence didn't seem to be at the core of his true preoccupation. He was a kind of old dandy, much more involved with his elegance than his well-being. A persistent and heavy smell of hashish hung over his hideaway.

Ali would pass by this shop on his way to and from school. Quite often he would hear music coming from within. Was the old man alternating the making of small-bone or wooden objects with the strumming of strings of some marvelous instrument?

One day, on his way back from school, Ali stood in the entryway to the shop, hypnotized by the music.

When the old man stopped playing, Ali was still there, fascinated and unable to budge. It was only when the old man motioned for him to come in that his legs could move again. The old man put the mandolin in his hands and guided his fingers. Ali was choking with the thickness of the smoke and the odors it spread.

He went back several times more, and gradually his fingers grew familiar with the chords; they became gentler, caressing. All by themselves, without the help of his eyes, they learned to find the complex tracks of the chords, the ones that lead to the heart of the notes, that elicit languorous laments, liberate imprisoned laughter, kindle the desire to dance or the thirst to go off to faraway places . . .

Now, with his eyes closed in spite of the thick semidarkness that might have absolved him, he abandons the world around him and returns to that merciful era. The mandolin resonates in his head. So close that by stretching out his hand he could touch it, Ali Elbouliga sees the sheath of his childhood again, his shell, distorted and annihilated by time. He belongs wholly to his instrument. Delight crosses his face, without the concentration, tense to the point of pain, of his beginnings. He has long since stopped grappling with his mandolin: he has become its brother and accomplice. Effort is no longer needed for harmony to unite the heart of the one and the heart of the other. They do not need light or a marked path to find each other again: it is enough to reach out your hand, to thrust your fingers into the dark to find communion.

Despite the time that has passed, the emotion is still there, covered over but ready to gush out, braving the harshness of the new period, braving the slogans and placards that are an invitation to destroy everything that gives rise to pure feeling, to make the world on earth into the dominion of devotion.

The summer
when time stopped

Boualem Yekker calls this season the last summer of reason. Sometimes, the last summer of history. Indeed, thereafter the country went freewheeling, leaving history behind.

Therefore, that summer was indeed the last. For, from then on, time had no seasons and no nuances. It had been transformed into a tunnel whose end could hardly be seen. Ever since, the sky had forsaken its luminosity; the sun had ceased to caress and tease languid bodies sensually, it had ceased shedding its gold to greet the new day and spattering the departing day with its blood.

That was the summer of attacks, but also of defiance. For a while now, bands of enlightened redeemers had been raiding the beaches, making life difficult for the summer visitors, going so far as to attack them physically. Women swimming by themselves were the obvious prey; they were tracked down, berated, and molested. A veritable psychosis set in and some beaches remained empty for a good part of the summer. But not everyone had surrendered. Insofar as one had the courage and was willing to accept the consequences, one could still resist.

Boualem Yekker was one of those who had decided to resist, those who had become aware that when the hordes confronting them had managed to spread their fear and impose silence they would have won. Thus, that summer, like all previous summers, he made preparations to go camping. His van, which served all year long to transport huge packages of books, was now dressing up, being transformed into a caravel heading merrily toward a vacation.

The crew consisted of Boualem, his wife Soraya, his daughter Kenza, his son Kamel, and Belka, the dog. The family had picked a place on the east coast, close to B——, without too many visitors, which they had discovered four years earlier and which twice before they had used as a camping ground. It was close to the lighthouse of Cape S——, on a dream site between the sea and the mountains, between rocks chewed up by the water and fir trees racing down slopes and steep paths. Going toward the shore there was a string of white rocks, resembling the giant vertebrae of a prehistoric monster. Beside that, a makeshift jetty and a dilapidated cabin, vestiges of a time when the changeover of the lighthouse was done by sea. A bit farther along, two gravelly streams, one of which sustained a smattering of vegetation.

These marvels constituted the daily horizon for the campers, who would often take the van to explore their surroundings, to vary and enrich their supply of images. They would pursue their treks as far up as the H—— Islands, which stood out in the distance of the interminable and quiet blue.

As for the beach, protected by a tall embankment and a row of pines, it was a perfect place for camping. The tent was pitched about fifty meters from the waves. Far from the capital city already besieged by groups preaching violence, the Yekker family thus spent three splendid weeks in which the only dark spot had been the marathon to the closest village, crawling with summer visitors and summer camps, to replenish their supplies. They had to fall all over each other to get bread, vegetables, cookies, and gasoline.

Later, Boualem would remember in great detail the day—September 1—that was to be the last of their vacation. You would have thought that nature itself had roughly obliterated the joyful, carefree mood of the night before. When the Yekkers came out of their tent early in the morning, heaven and earth were competing in their display of anger and sadness.

The sea raised a turbulent surface on which three thick bands, gigantic strips, stood out, going from antimony blue to bilious green. The wind was prodding a lazy herd of clouds across the sky, some opaque, some translucent, in shapes that were threatening, good-natured, or crazy. Fantastic constructions were sketched and then undone. In the resulting rifts, floods of sunlight came streaming through. The shadows projected by the clouds were like gaping wounds in the earth.

Accompanied by his son, Boualem had gone to take a walk in the fields, a kind of farewell visit to this charming place, this haven of calm. The spot had become a part of their life, even incarnating the most

carefree and most subtle side of that life. It was an en-
clave of serenity in a country that was growing more
ensnared in extremism and violence by the day.

Moistened by the light rain that had fallen at
dawn, the fields gave off a smell of humus. Father
and son walked in silence through the tall, dry grass.
The rain had been no help at all to the roots and
stalks that had hardened in the scorching heat,
where no nerve or living fiber pulsed or trembled; it
was as if someone had done his best to soak a skele-
ton with water.

The dog had followed them at a distance and
then caught up with them. Now she was trotting
ahead of them, unrestrained, coming and going as
her curiosity dictated. Her flanks, belly, and paws
were covered with tiny dry seeds, minuscule hedge-
hogs curled up in her silky thickness. The trousers of
her companions had harvested their share of clingy
vegetation, tiny fledgling arrows. Kamel's were light-
colored and the dusty wet stalks had thoroughly
traced them with muddy streaks going in every
direction.

The rain had begun to fall again, gently, and the
two strollers ran for shelter beneath the foliage of

the olive trees standing in a line less than a hundred meters away. As they ran they stirred up a pair of turtle-doves that flew away noisily in a vibration of feathers. When they stopped on the edge of a dried-up brook, the adolescent cried out: two martens were romping about below, teasing each other and rolling around in the earth nipped by the rain. Suddenly aware of human presence, they interrupted their frolicking and fled into a thicket.

The two men felt their hearts leap; seeing this simple and wild display was like a miracle. It was the first time either of them had seen a marten. The dog had disappeared and both found it strange that it wasn't she who had flushed out the wild animals. Before they even reached the olive trees, the rain stopped again. Boualem looked up at the sky. Its wings motionless, a falcon was letting itself be carried by the wind, drifting among the grayish clouds.

Today, everything was heralding fall, with its tender light, benevolent even in its sadness, its colors resting from having danced, shimmered, and glowed too much throughout the two preceding seasons. Nature would soon lay down her gleaming armor, take off her parade costume to slip on some indoor garment, more intimate and modest.

The two men went back to the campground. Preparations for the return trip were quickly made, but the family lingered to watch the stormy sea churned up by the east wind. Kamel had been told by fishermen that this wind, which they called the three-six-nine, would not stop for three days at least, or else not for a number of days that was a multiple of three.

It was on the road, about fifty kilometers before they arrived in the capital city, that they ran into an unusual roadblock set up by some bearded young men, rigged out like Afghan warriors but with a flight of fancy introduced by the union of upscale sneakers and pajamas, gandouras and leather jackets. Armed with bludgeons and swords, but also with automatic pistols and even submachine guns, they were stopping cars and looking inside, lingering on the clothing of the riders, especially of the women.

Two cars had been forced to park and their passengers, having been ordered to get out, were engaged in vigorous discussion with some menacing bearded men, who seemed to be particularly hostile to three young women whose beachwear was barely covered up by their flimsy dresses.

Long after having passed the barricade, Boualem Yekker was still trembling with indignation. His throat was tight with a bitter feeling of helplessness. Most devastating was the paralyzing cowardice that had taken hold of everyone, he himself being no exception.

Pilgrim of the new times

The streetlights, which stay on and mark the roads with their shy eyes hurt by the sun's splendor, are one of the few traces that still recall the former regime.

Boualem Yekker looks at the orange balls, anachronistic fruits blooming at the crown of the poles. He is wondering just what department is responsible for the lighting and how much the cost of this waste of energy is to what was once the Republic, and which now calls itself the Community in the Faith. It amuses him to come up with a subject to reflect on every now and then, an entertaining theme that pulls him far away from the present.

He is trying not to think about what may await him at the end of his route. In the end, will he even find the batch of books he is going to pick up? A semiclandestine circuit exists, sustained by a ring with a foreign network, where one can stock up on "profane" publications. But, besides the fact that the quantities brought into circulation are insufficient, the conversion of local money into foreign currency, as well as the different transaction taxes, make books nearly unobtainable. A work by Maupassant, Steinbeck, Mohammed Dib, or Hermann Hesse costs half the monthly salary of a manual laborer. The Community's Department of Control tolerates the irregularities of this circuit, first of all because it is highly marginal, and then because financially it penalizes those who like "inappropriate" reading material. As soon as the modest Community closes its eyes to drugs and prostitution, it can certainly show itself to be broad-minded where devious but inoffensive readers are concerned. Even in the centuries when this Faith was at its high point and, a star without any rivals, would illuminate the world inspired by devotion, did not a depraved literature exist that celebrated the body and drinking, provoking doubts and questions? A literature whose importance was exaggerated by certain ill-intentioned minds, placing it on a pedestal so that it would overshadow the other literature, the one wholly reserved for the celebration of the Creator and the explanation of His Word?

Boualem Yekker h
orange globes. He is th
Republic just before t
the different politica
were confronting each other.
As he was being questioned about his reading, the
man who today holds the post of Vizier of Reflection,
answered that he forbade himself any reading other
than the Holy Book; that novels, essays, and other
perverse ramblings were nothing but fancy notions
he disdained and whose accounts he would settle
on the day that the Almighty, keeper of the secret
of hierarchies, gave him the opportunity. At the
time, Boualem Yekker could not prevent himself
from noticing the abyss that separated him—who
had read some thousand books or more from Plato
to Kawabata, by way of Mohammed Iqbal, Kazteb
Yacine, Octavio Paz, and Kafka—from the man who,
never having consulted any book, aspired to govern
the country. And who is governing it today.

The road is clear. The new working hours, regu-
lated by the rhythm of the prayers, have created new
traffic patterns: gridlock at ungodly hours, and traffic flowing freely at unexpected moments. Another
aspect of the new mores: huge Mercedes parked in

g lines near the mosques. Millionaires of every kind have discovered religious fervor. Among the believing masses and at a small price, they have acquired a respectability that erases all their activities and launders their money.

Boualem Yekker notices a young man, half hidden by a dense row of parked cars, trying to hitch a ride. He goes toward him as he slows down, thinking deep inside that perhaps he is about to commit a reckless act. In fact, as a security measure he has stopped picking up hitchhikers; for those citizens—freethinkers and intellectuals—who have declared themselves against the establishment of the Community regime, and who are identified agnostics, are still being sought by the Vigilant Brothers' militias. And Boualem Yekker, who knows that his activities as a bookseller are hanging by the thinnest of threads, prefers to avoid being seen in the company of a suspicious person, just as he takes care to avoid contact with people (the place is teeming with spies and agitators) who could complicate his life.

So why does he stop this time? He cannot explain it. Is it the young man's wretched look and his shipwrecked demeanor calling for help that have made Boualem decide to stop? Is his imagination, in its fever of excitement, playing a trick on him by introducing the hitchhiker to him in a guise that isn't really his?

With a very heavy limp, the young man approaches the car hobbling and gets in next to Boualem Yekker. He arranges his gandoura under his legs as women do before they sit down, then holds out his hand and says:

"May God reward you with kindness."

They remain silent for a time. Questions are whirling around inside Boualem Yekker's head. Was he right to let this individual get into his car? Should he make conversation with him or just let things take their course? Should he not perhaps make up for his carelessness and look for a subterfuge to rid himself as quickly as possible of this passenger?

Furtively, the two men observe each other in silence, as if the first word they might exchange was bound to have drastic consequences and neither of them dared to take the responsibility for pronouncing it. Boualem Yekker ends up by telling himself that, as a well-mannered host, it is up to him to put his passenger at ease and initiate the discussion, thereby breaking through this icy wall. A passerby unexpectedly comes to his aid, by rushing out of an adjacent alley and hastily crossing in front of him. Boualem slams on the brakes with a violent shrieking of tires. Forcing himself to control his anger, he says:

"People don't remember how to act in city streets. They don't know what a pedestrian crosswalk is anymore. They cut across any old way, with total contempt for all the rules, as if they were coming out into the desert, into the middle of a vacuum."

"You shouldn't spurn the desert. It is the place of every Revelation. It is the cradle of the prophecies."

"In my opinion, people your age should be interested in things other than the prophecies."

"And in what, exactly, if you please?"

"There are so many things of interest: sports, art, science, cooking."

"Cooking is women's business. Art is nothing but a pretentious endeavor and it is impious to compete with His Work. As for science, is that not wholly contained in His Omniscience? All knowledge finds its source in our religion."

"Did you study?"

"Of course. I went as far as the year of the *baccalauréat*. I have a gift for theology and Arabic literature. It was foreign languages and worldly sciences that closed the doors of the university for me."

"Still, you have heard about the theorem of Thales and the theorem of Pythagoras. Those are formulas that were established many centuries before Jesus Christ, and thus even more centuries before our religion made its appearance."

The young man does not answer. He turns his back to the driver and looks out the lowered window as if he were searching for a response in the distance. A woman, dressed in black but with her face and head uncovered, comes toward them on the sidewalk. When they have passed her, the young man chides:

"There is much work to be done yet to bring this people back onto the straight path. Shamelessness is displayed in broad daylight without anyone denouncing it."

"Do you feel personally involved in everyone's behavior?"

"Did our Prophet—may Salvation and Prayer be His—not say: 'Each one of you is a shepherd and every shepherd will account for his herd'?"

"And the herd you watch is the immense herd of humanity! Is that not a bit too much for you?"

"In fact, humanity is a herd floundering around in the muck of debauchery and the darkness of agnosticism. Our efforts to make it rediscover the light

41

shall not be in vain. Why do you look so skeptical about the chances of Good being triumphant? Are you, too, overwhelmed with doubt?"

"I'm just talking with you. I am a solitary old man, and I turn out to be rather talkative and even rather irritating every time I run into a man as understanding as you, who shows himself to be disposed to listening to me."

"So you have no family?"

Boualem Yekker remains silent. He again sees the afternoon when the cord that had been stretched too far had finally broken. His wife was standing before him, dressed in black from top to toe, her body denied and erased by the stiff and rigid fabric. Her wish to survive exuded violently from her eyes, which were all that the shroud-shaped fabric had left visible. The children had taken their mother's side; they, too, were unwilling to live the life of outcasts and pariahs; they were prepared to do without the sap and challenges of real life in order to conform to the new norm and continue to exist under the new implacable and castrating order. It was proper to act in emulation of all the neighbors: let your beard grow, wear a gandoura, and display overwhelming piety. But Boualem had been unwavering; he resisted these mutilating compromises with all his might; his opinion of life was too high for him to make do with its shadow, its wrapping, and its peelings. He was determined to brave anything: contempt, solitude, and vexations in order to continue to honor the things and ideas he believed in. And the fatal break occurred.

The young hitchhiker makes himself right at home. He lies back on the seat, his legs horizontally extended, his sandaled feet wedged beneath the glove compartment. One might say that he has just irrefutably established the proof of his superiority over the person to whom, just a few moments earlier, he was indebted for having picked him up from the street. This gentleman, who he was weak enough to think had acted out of the love of Good, undoubtedly is just one of those cynics who adore materialist thinking—for quite obviously there still are followers of sacrilege in the country that has found its way back to God. The young man decides to be merciless, for the triumph of Good requires it!

"Excuse me, Uncle, but to me you seem beleaguered by the confusion of those who are lacking in faith. I apologize in advance, for I hope that I am wrong."

"Son, it is a risky business to set oneself up as the judge of others, for one is mistaken more often than should be allowed."

"He who preaches truth is not mistaken; he often encounters adversity, but error does not lie on his path."

This rock-driven certainty, having become the basis for all reasoning today, brings back the memory of some of the last discussions he had with his son. Kamel, worked over by his school and neighborhood, had finally yielded to the pressure. With head down, he joined the group cooped up in the meadow of certitude. He refused to be branded and, for that reason, decided to play the game. He had made it very clear that he did not need a father whose target of sarcasm and pillory he would be . . .

The zealous passenger, now feeling he had a mission, goes back on the attack.

"We have grappled hard with the invincible power of the lie. We didn't even believe that one day we would be victorious: the Almighty supported us. We must show ourselves to be worthy of His assistance by spreading His light everywhere."

"Do you have a fiancée?" Boualem asks him, suddenly feeling the need to be less formal.

The man opposite him blushes as if he had been caught.

"Those things are too personal and shouldn't be discussed in public."

"So, then, in your congregation everything essential bears the stamp of shame?"

The young man is taken aback. Suddenly he seems preoccupied. He looks around in every direction.

"I'd like to get out over there, across from the vegetable vendor," he says nervously.

Before he leaves the car, he bends toward Boualem and, with a half-distressed, half-threatening look, whispers right into his face:

"Fear God, oh man whose white hair has not brought him wisdom and repentance. Punishment shall be terrible and never-ending."

Then he moves away, hobbling but decisively, as if he were going toward a great moment in history.

The Good whose substance the Almighty established

The first stone that hit him was thrown by a girl. Twelve years old, maybe, no more. But a girl already ripe, a person of the present time, settled into the limpid logic of exclusion and stoning. At the bottom of her little heart, she is completely blameless. She is on the side of the new right: the side that allows you, without remorse, to exclude those who do not share your convictions.

Boualem Yekker leaves the bookstore just to stretch his legs and take a look at the outside world. There has not been a single customer or visitor all day. Tired of sitting, as well as of the back-and-forth between cash register and shelves, he wants to breathe some fresh air. It is as if they have been waiting for him for a long time, with a clever trap. For the stone comes right away. It is followed by a second one, and then a third. Then the stone throwers show themselves, arrogant and aggressive, defying him from the distance with waving arms and raucous and belligerent cries. Before the group disappears into a downhill alleyway, the girl, who looks as if she is the initiator and the leader, hoists herself on the tips of her toes and shouts:

"May God destroy you, you heathen!"

The stone did not hurt him, having hit his shoulder where it was cushioned by the thickness of his corduroy jacket. He hesitates for a moment, overcome by the desire to pursue them or, at least, to return their threats. But he does nothing. He calmly goes back into the bookstore as if nothing had happened. Nevertheless, he wonders if these precocious persecutors are acting on their own accord as future citizens, models of redemption, or if some adult inspired them.

Exactly five days earlier, he found the windshield of his car shattered and one tire slashed with a knife—damage that is all the more irreparable in that the parts are not available on the regular market and obtaining them takes weeks of research, contacts, and negotiations. Are these children today the same ones who vandalized his car? It is only a conjecture, but he knows that the adolescents being made into fanatics in the mosques are trained to jump at your throat like Dobermans, and are capable of anything, of sacrifice as well as of crime, of abnegation as well as of terrorism. They carry death within them, ready to inflict it as well as to turn it against themselves without so much as raising an eyebrow. Did not the one who runs the country, in charge of theology and politics, state on television a few days ago, "What we want is not power but martyrdom"? He immediately added: "Our only earthly dream is to bring out into the light what the darkness hides. We cannot go around the darkness, that would be failing in our mission, which consists of enlightening. There are men who want to go on living inside our borders while they refuse to be enlightened. Do we have the right before God to leave these men bogged down in the cesspool of error?"

Children have become the blind and convinced executors of a truth that has been presented to them as a higher truth. They have nothing on this earth: no material goods, no culture, no leisure activities, no affection, no hopes; their horizons are blocked. They are ready to kill and to die. Of what use is life, they are asked, when true existence awaits them elsewhere, outside of this world of injustice and sin, an existence they should especially not jeopardize by their hesitations or their "disobedience" here below? They must serve the Truth, break the barriers of arbitrary and fallacious human law in order to attain and serve true morality, the one that eludes time and circumstances because it is the emanation of the Good whose outlines and substance have been established once and for all by the Almighty.

Boualem Yekker is no longer able to find comfort among the books surrounding him. Something has been deeply ruptured. It is as if he has suddenly discovered an irreparable breach separating his body of book learning from his body of flesh. It is the latter that receives the stones of injustice and hatred, that twists with pain or moans. The first body can be compared to a head wandering around in the clouds, in benign regions where landscapes are not aggressive and where stones cause no injuries.

After the first sense of indifference caused by surprise has passed, his body begins to shake with indignation. Books no longer protect him, for they too have been rejected and humiliated by the value system and the new order. Boualem Yekker feels helpless again, holds back the rage and tears of a child watching his humiliated father submit to the hu-

miliation in silence. Still, books have unnerved the
world, shaken it like a tree that is forced to render its
fruit! Looking at his shelves, Boualem Yekker has the
depressing sense that books have forsaken their im-
pudence, that they have turned into extras hugging
the walls. They have covered their faces with veils.
Out of shame and bitter disappointment. Boualem
is no longer able to locate his most enduring companions, those thick bound volumes of ancient times,
amassing centuries and years without losing any of
their power and acumen.

With stones they have chased him away from
those volumes with their familiar and restful smell
and grain, the smell of trenchant wisdom, the grain
of the leather across which so many days and so many
hands have passed without changing it in any way.

Will the children leave him in peace or will they
come back sometime soon, full of the same brutality
and with even more harmful stones? His newly
awakened senses are highly charged. He waits like
an animal on the lookout, impervious to the span of
time, as if time were trivial in the face of the prey's
significance.

All of a sudden, he hears a noise. A real noise, not
an invention of his overexcited senses. His nerves

jump as if they had been stripped bare. He doesn't know what attitude he should take; he is afraid he won't be able to control himself. Is he going to fly off the handle at the risk of making himself ridiculous or even of committing some deplorable act, or is he going to submit and drink humiliation down to the dregs?

The sound—of footsteps—comes closer. Ali Elbouliga slowly pushes the door open. Boualem Yekker stops himself from running over and kissing him, so thrilled is he to find an ally in this moment of adversity. His fear and uneasiness vanish. The world wears a human face again.

His emotion keeps him from speaking the words and thoughts that crowd inside his head like a panicked herd. Yet, he is visibly happy, a flame lights him from within, a beneficent flow rushes through him. Unable to stay in place, he gets up and goes to meet Ali Elbouliga, something he has never done before. He barely checks himself from embracing him, which would have surprised, if not terrified, poor Elbouliga, who might well have thought the bookseller had gone mad.

Without a word, Boualem Yekker goes to a shelf where he immerses himself in looking at some titles, as if he wants Elbouliga to think he did not get up for him. Having mastered his emotion, he goes back and sits down behind the tiny desk.

In his quiet voice, Ali Elbouliga says, almost inaudibly:

"I've heard that for every district they're making lists of people to be neutralized or punished, activities to be stopped, and businesses to be closed. It seems this will affect everyone and everything: artists, teachers, sports clubs, restaurants where they suspect alcohol is being served on the sly, hotels they consider immoral, and bookstores.

"It's been a long time since any committee of propriety has initiated this kind of censorship. It's the perfect opportunity to settle a few accounts. The new leaders are most inventive in matters of absurdity."

Standing on a stepladder, Boualem Yekker busies himself with some books, moving them around just to be occupied with something and to put some distance between himself and Ali, for he senses that he is about to confess something he cannot say to his face, for fear that Ali might see his trembling lips and his face twisting with nervous tics.

Calm but pale, he says at last in a monotone, "I was attacked today."

"What sort of attack?"

"Children assaulted me."

"Children you know?"

"I'm not altogether sure. Lately, on three separate occasions, children have stopped in front of the shopwindow and started looking at the books. Each time I was ecstatic, for it had been a long time since something like that had happened. But each time, as soon as I came out to ask the children whether I could help them look for something, they took to their heels. Were they the same children who attacked me? They were too far away for me to know."

"You're not overdramatizing this a little?"

"I'm mostly afraid they'll come back to break the window."

"Children are very involved in the 'civilizing' work the new masters of the country are undertaking. They often assist the adults in volunteer work, propaganda missions, and even in punitive operations."

"I do hope they won't come back. I really have no idea how I'd react. I cannot remain passive in the face of violence and injustice—especially when they are directed against me."

Outside, the light has lost its glow and grown soft to the point of gloom. It is almost dark in the bookstore. But Boualem Yekker is careful not to turn on the lights. Today, against all expectation, Ali Elbouliga's presence consoles and comforts him, but he would rather not see his face—any more than he wants to be seen by Ali.

The nocturnal tribunal

As soon as he has taken the highway exit leading to the capital's center, Boualem Yekker, seeing the compact mass of the city plunge down toward the sea, is struck by the way the buildings look. They are lopsided. Has there been an earthquake while he was gone? That seems unlikely, for he would have heard about it on the radio (he rarely watches TV). With utmost surprise, he also notices that the course of the road he knows so well has undergone some changes; this major road he is taking leads straight to the harbor, not around the city on the southern end as it should go.

Is it possible for a city to be completely transformed in a few days' time? The flow of cars is unpredictable: at times the road is empty, and at other times cars come bolting down in tightly packed lines. One might say it is being controlled by one of those gadgets on electronic games that create profusion or a blank, depending on the manipulation.

Suddenly, Boualem Yekker is forced to slow down. An interminable traffic jam has formed in front of him; despite all his efforts, he cannot see where it ends. His gradual slowdown soon turns into a complete standstill. Following the example of many drivers already in deep conversation, he gets out of the car to make some inquiries. He approaches a group. To his great astonishment, the men are discussing a subject that has nothing to do with the situation; one is boasting about the quality of the olive oil from Akbou in Lesser Kabylia; another is defending the virtues of colza oil, recently imported and sold in all the country's supermarkets. Not knowing how to enter the conversation, Boualem Yekker moves away in the direction of another group of people, well groomed and almost all of them wearing glasses. Rational and educated people, is Boualem Yekker's guess, hoping they will provide him with invaluable information about the blockage. As he comes closer, he hears their debate: the one speaking is questioning the usefulness of social sciences in a developing country that has not yet mastered technology. A woman with short hair is jumping up and down and clearing her throat, eager to contradict what has been said.

Deep despair comes over Boualem Yekker. Might he be the object of a conspiracy? In any event, he understands that he must find out on his own what has caused this monstrous traffic jam, stretching out like a python barring access to the city.

He walks away from his car in search of an explanation. Like him, other drivers are moving forward toward the head of the metal python. Then, about fifty meters in front of him, he notices some men with hoods who are roughly dragging passengers out of their cars and pinning them, their hands raised, against the overheated metal. Boualem Yekker goes toward them; he is not afraid; rebellion and indignation engulf him, leaving no room for any other feeling. He almost steps on a dog lying quietly in the shade of a truck, oblivious to the chaos and the agitation of humans. For a brief moment, Boualem wishes he were that carefree dog, or any other animal for that matter. How blissful it would be to escape from the laws and abuses of a humanity that is more deranged than ever, capable of any and all excesses and perversions.

When he reaches the commando unit checking

the cars, three men swoop down on him, encircle him, and throw him to the ground. As he continues to fight back and return their blows, the hood of one of the men falls off and exposes the face of his son. Kamel's beard, suddenly freed, flows down like black water, drawing a curtain over his neck. Confronted with the discovery, Boualem Yekker stands dumbfounded. His body feels paralyzed. One of the two men attacking him takes advantage of his stupefaction to punch him violently in the head with his fist.

He wakes up in a kind of ambulant barracks, a strangely silent canvas camp in which only mysterious and worrisome shadows slither in and out. Boualem Yekker tries to get up, but his body is tied to a cot by the ankles, wrists, and thighs. He is all alone in the tent: no other prisoner, no guard. He wonders what he should do, what response might be the least detrimental to him: call out or remain quiet? Lie there motionless or try to undo his bonds? His mind is too foggy, the conflicting thoughts inside his head unable to focus or affix themselves. He is incapable of holding on to a decision. Something has happened that his intelligence is wearing itself out trying to define. Willingly, he lets himself slide into a kind of lethargy, waiting to better understand. He remains at the borderline between sleep and wakefulness, every now and then through an opening in the tent venturing a glance at the night, illuminated by a ballet of stars, and, for the first time perhaps, he wonders whether those cold, distant sparkles really have an impact on the vagaries of human life.

A guard, in the strange getup they call "Afghan," ducks into the tent. He bends down over Boualem Yekker's tied up and aching body and, without a word, begins to undo the straps. Once his body has been freed, the prisoner is roughly pulled upright and pushed out with a heavy machine gun.

Outside, the night is cool and Boualem Yekker begins to tremble, not quite knowing whether he trembles with cold or with fear. The tent he enters is spacious. A man with an enormous turban is enthroned more than a meter above everyone else.

Boualem Yekker is led between the silent rows to the other end of the tent, where men in chains are waiting on their knees. He is the only one in the group whose limbs are not tied. Why, among the other accused, is he so privileged? He thinks he knows the reason when he sees Kamel standing right behind the emir-judge, half hidden in the semidarkness. Before he has time to wonder about anything further, one of his companions in misfortune has been pushed before the emir. A blazing light from an invisible projector is brutally shed on the accused, who huddles down beneath the powerful halo, like a beast surrounded by hunters.

His wrinkled face twitches nervously. His sweat beads here and there and then is stopped, prisoner to the folds of his flesh. The man stammers, gesticulates, gets tangled in his attempt to control his voice, master his emotion, and find the right words, the expression that will be convincing. As he begins to speak, his voice grows more and more assured, the pitch rises higher and clearer.

"Emir-judge, Sir, oh your Holiness! I have never said that you were not right. Such judgments, God be thanked, never touched my spirit, not even during my moments of distraction or in the terrifying dreams that inhabit the darkness of my cell. What distresses me, but what I accept submissively, for your Sagacity cannot be mistaken, is the obstinacy in transferring other problems onto the one concerning me, in which nobody here or elsewhere could have any interest . . ."

The accused stops, out of breath, his hands and

chin shaking. He opens his mouth; he appears to be about to speak, but it is several moments before the first syllables come out.

"Mister Governor, excuse me, Imam-Judge, Sir, what I also find hard to understand is the mania for overloading everything—may God condemn me if I hold you responsible for that. What good is it to have a surplus of witnesses, when what I myself have admitted far outweighs their accusations? You have heard their stream of invectives and obscure insinuations. In reality, all they are doing is complicating and obscuring a matter that is, nevertheless, very clear. I am going to end up thinking—forgive me for such inordinate arrogance—that there is a true conspiracy against me. Yet, I am the only one who knows in every last detail what I have done from start to finish—He who hears and sees everything having been my only witness. My intention is to facilitate your task to the maximum, Sir Imam-Judge. I will not only reveal my acts but my plans as well, which the Almighty did not permit me to accomplish. Therefore, I do not understand—and again I implore you to grant me absolution for my insolence—how the respectable and infallible organization whose devoted and clear-sighted leader you are can seek to complicate my case with such twisted and inappropriate depositions from witnesses . . ."

The rest of his speech is drowned out by the booing of the audience. But the emir-judge imposes silence with a mere flash of his eyes. With a finger raised to heaven, he magnanimously erases the mistake and absolves the wretched orator, who is still mumbling and wringing his hands, trying in one and the same sentence to deal a blow to the arguments and ask for pardon.

It is Boualem Yekker's turn to come before the emir-judge. Since the audience has begun to talk, stamp its feet, and boo again, Boualem cannot hear the main charges against him. He desperately strains his ears, hoping to catch some of the imam-judge's rapid-fire words, just one word to hang on to as to a life jacket or a flare. A kind of mush, syllables jolting against each other and running together, seems to be coming from the dignitary's mouth. Exasperated, Boualem Yekker feels like shouting at the audience to be quiet, but that requires an audacity he doesn't dare allow himself. And he is not at all certain his voice will even carry. Overwhelmed, he lowers his head, clinging to the faint hope that the emir may repeat his indictment when the room is quiet.

At that moment, Kamel takes a step forward. He is looking into the distance, as if his father's presence among the accused is of no concern to him. He catches sight of a young man hidden among the people and, in an authoritarian voice, begins shouting at him. When the man he shouts at is slow in reacting to his command, Kamel jumps off the podium, crosses the room in double-quick time, and pulls his unlucky victim out of the human mass. Without hesitation, he drags him forward, laying into him all the while. A few protestations rise from the crowd. Then everything grows silent, the protesters suddenly realizing they could well receive the same treatment.

A reckless idea, verging on madness, enters Boualem Yekker's head. He no longer recognizes that cruel and dehumanized human being, corrupted by he knows not what organization, as his son. He even tells himself that, having fathered Kamel, it is his responsibility to deliver society from him.

Kamel continues his bullying and his poor victim begins now to resist by grasping at objects, protesting, and calling out. As Kamel drags the man toward the emir-judge, a plan takes shape inside the father's head. Very close to him, preoccupied with and entertained by the spectacle, one of the guards is no longer paying attention to the prisoners. A submachine gun is tucked inside his broad belt, within hand's reach of Boualem Yekker.

When Kamel, still manhandling his victim, reaches the first row, his father throws himself at the weapon, grabs it, adjusts it, and empties the magazine. In five seconds, everything is over. Kamel collapses without a cry. His father, whom nobody in the tent seeks to arrest, bends over him. With heartbreaking sorrow, he watches the impassive and bearded mask his son has been wearing fall nearby, mangled by bullets. Kamel's real face has appeared, the face of an adolescent, beardless and fresh, without any trace of a wound . . .

The dying boy's hands reach out to his father and, before breathing his last, he utters laboriously:

"Our life has been nothing but a gaping wound swarming with the maggots of delusion."

Boualem Yekker wakes up feverishly, his face flooded with tears. The side he has slept on is completely numb. He listens to a bird chirping in the lemon tree in the courtyard.

The binding text

Boualem is very fond of Arabic texts with their loose
punctuation, texts that know no quotation marks
and where all voices hold dialogues and blend. Long
discursive spirals. An abstraction of letters curved in
a veritable geometry of bas-relief. A language that is
abstract in itself, despite the burden of words and
their sounds meant to awaken the bogged-down
memory. You have to be on your guard at all times,
a vigilant reader, to reestablish the lines from the
meaning, to mark out the territory from the phrases,
to take apart the coiled-up paragraphs. Each time
the reading is a new adventure, unpredictable steps
forward, convoluted comings and goings to flush
out the face of the words, give them back their pur-
pose, place them in their role of locomotive or car-
riage. It is a hesitant and prudent reading in which
you try to avoid misleading or rambling paths.

Sometimes, words drag you along like impatient

dogs and, out of breath and stumbling, you are forced to follow. Should the route prove to be long you begin to be distracted by a multitude of diverging, intertwining, or crumbling paths. You hesitate and become concerned, but at the end of the course you manage to rein in the restive words that have raced along. They stop rearing and pawing the ground, meekly come to a standstill, and stretch their necks out to Boualem, who ascribes meanings and roles to them. They become companions once more, lanterns lighting the planet and unveiling its wonders. Letters that are cursive or hooked, plump or spindly. Letters that are populated with a whimsical menagerie.

Every time Boualem picks up one of these books with its hooked or conjoined letters, he sees himself at the Koranic school again. The words—so sweet you would want to caress them—wind around each other, inoffensive snakes, and get tangled up on the kaolin-soaked board. The *smakh* (an ink whose base is burned wool) weeps over the white surface, at the beck and call of the reed pen scratching as it moves along. When the board is covered at last (you had to bend over it, stick your tongue out, and housebreak the recalcitrant fingers) it becomes a carpet of scrolls, lines, curves whose color goes from black to dark brown, depending on the thickness of the ink. You have to learn the sura by heart and then wash the board (turned grayish where the alphabet, the water, and the kaolin came together) in order to write other suras down. Plowing and sowing begun anew.

The child is crushed beneath the board, its panoply of secrets, threats, and dictates. The child is terrorized by the old teacher with his slow-moving voice and his quick stick, infallible and merciless. The dozing old teacher knows so many prescriptions for the hereafter, he has formulas that absolve and formulas that obliterate, words that prune down to the bone, making you bleed. The flies, too, are dozing; they fly around reluctantly and, when they settle on a dirty cheek or a runny nostril, they stay there despite threatening gestures.

Bathing in sweat. Sometimes the teacher actually falls fast asleep. A delightful moment of freedom for the young reciters who transform their boards into shields and their *galam* into javelins. An aviary class where the teacher springs up with a start, briefly alarmed to see himself assailed by a band of braying and threatening barbarians, then gradually coming back to reality until he has taken control of the situation again. He takes possession of his domain with a first hit of his stick, haphazardly leaving stripes on jutting sides, shaven skulls, lazy hands or legs (more nimble extremities have learned to avoid the blows and to move out of the way).

The Text bombarded with the blows of a stick. Learning—droning delivery—by suffering. Maxims—divine words swallowed like a potion grazing the palate. Boualem wants to devote himself to something else, not only to escape this oppression but also to take revenge. He has to find a subterfuge. Stop the stars at the hour the night consumes the world? Purify the planet by setting it aflame with the scorching heat? Dreams twist and turn. There is no place to hide. The room where the teacher holds court contains no closet, no trunk, no shady corner—just two niches dug into the wall. An uncompromising nakedness and light—like those of the Word taught by the man with the stick. Imagination is eroded by the Truth blocking the horizon, preventing eye and mind from roaming beyond the assigned limits. The child is seriously trapped. Desire to shut himself away, to resist so that the castrating Truth will not advance, destroying gladness, impertinence, and fantasy. A dream quickly disintegrating under the stick that comes crashing down.

Little Boualem wants to see the world. He wants to desert the jail-class. He is miserable knowing that these sessions devoted to the voiceless adoration of the Truth are shielding him from an exciting universe, a universe that is both bewitching and dangerous, in which playful noises coexist with cars, marvelous animals, and moaning ships going to the open sea. Stirring about in this multifaceted universe, turning like a noria, are sages and fools, good people and perverse and dangerous individuals, men who preach and others who shout and curse. This kaleidoscope universe is teeming with nourishing, cooling, and shade-bringing trees, decorative plants, caged birds and free-flying birds connected by their love of song, cafés where people talk and laugh, places where they have a good time and dance. You only have to leave the jail-school to rush into this spinning universe.

Boualem wants to leave the arid and lifeless season of the Text to plunge into other seasons in which heat follows upon cold, plants change their finery, colors explode and then grow dull, and the sky is a painting in perpetual upheaval. He aspires to tasting the succulence of the planet!

Little Boualem tells himself that it is a good thing to listen to God's Word, but that if He has given us a chest with an impatient heart, legs, fingers, eyes, and a tongue somewhat cramped in its cage of teeth, it is for us to use and test them.

Vaguely, the child suspects that the verses will not help him grow. He would like to travel the world. What he needs are elegant and colorful clothes, horses, boats, houses whose facades are lit up and turned off, and signs promising adventure. The verses that mark the path to Paradise appear too harsh to him, they discourage the imagination and clip the wings of dreams. Boualem wants songs of departure, lamentations that speak of nostalgia and the sorrow of man lost in the cities of exile. What comes to his mind as well—and with what excitement and embarrassment!—are the songs dedicated to the women one desires.

But it is not only the teacher who stands between adventure and himself, it is all of society, blinded and fanaticized by the Text, a society tethered to a Word that pulverizes it.

A dream shaped like madness

A man and a woman in the street, deeply engrossed in a friendly discussion. She has no wish to avoid him. He, the brute guided by his sex, does not think of throwing himself on her and knocking her down. She is not hiding her face because she fears that might awaken the beast in him. He does not flee from her because he fears the devil in him might control his decisions.

Boualem Yekker is thinking of scenes that once were normal and natural, of men and women having discussions like human beings with reason, restraint, and consideration; people capable of friendship, affection, respect, civic responsibility, and anger—men and women so vastly different from the watchful beasts they have since become to each other.

From inside his bookstore, through the triangle cut by the open door, he watches black shapes, the hermetically sealed fabric that leaves no trace whatever of a human body. Women are hiding inside, cursed beings of temptation and lust to be ignored by the eye of the believer. Sometimes he sees couples pass by, a strange togetherness of two people who avow no bond; the man, most often bearded, restricted by his hybrid garb of gandoura and jacket or an overcoat; the woman, entirely invisible inside her black tower.

Sometimes it happens that the books get on his nerves. He knows they are his window on the world, but he is also aware that he is their prisoner. The idea has frequently occurred to him—an idea he knows to be unrealizable—to burn both his personal library and his bookstore. He has no doubt that he would be delivered this way, like someone who rids himself of a tyrannical father or mother. He also gets away from books sometimes to pay attention to other things—as he is doing today to the people passing by in the street, trying to check out women or couples in particular.

Couples! Can you really speak of couples in a society split in two, where one half is erased from view, denied, reduced to a receptacle, a place of pleasure in the guilt-ridden darkness?

It is true that in this country the attitude has

never been conciliatory toward women. They have been condemned to hard work, bullying, and sarcastic remarks. Work in the fields and in the house, the many tasks and beatings: they have been spared nothing. But the woman was present, carried her weight with all her charm, all her determination, and all her suffering. She was the locality of the ordeal; she was the center of a drama woven of poverty, greed, jealousy, love, desire, and the struggle that each new day would impose. Woman was abused, but not, like today, reduced to some shameful thing to be hidden behind a black veil. In no way did she correspond to this object of seduction and damnation from whom the believer must be safeguarded as if from a lure of the devil. Today women are at the core of the sermons in most of the places of worship: in the same way as artists, atheists, and freethinkers, they are mentioned as the source of our manifold miseries, the cause of the righteous punishment that overwhelms us. If God refuses to pour his riches, his compassion, and his blessing out over us, is it not because of these entertainers, these depraved ones, these sins incarnate whose existence itself constitutes an offense to Heaven? The preachers, once in full form, lose all sense of measure and toss in excessive amounts of execrating and murderous formulas. Boualem Yekker has always been appalled at the idea that God should have to put up with such despicable representatives. The grand invention that lately has been feeding endless debates in the mosques stipulates that, when the time—blessed by God—comes to service one's wife in the dark, it is the believer's duty to get into bed with the right foot first, otherwise Satan will get there before him! He must also accomplish the act while lying on his right side.

In the oppressive city where he used to live and still lives, Boualem Yekker had put together dreams— oh, he no longer dares to do so—about the ideal city where he would like to live and watch his children blossom. First there would be greenery—trees and lawns—much greenery that would provide shade, coolness, fruits, the music of leaves, and shelter for love. There would be creators of beauty, rhythms, idylls, buildings, and machines. But there was no place at all for coordinators of the faith, supervisors of conscience, guardians of morality, and those establishing the power of Heaven. Boualem Yekker yearned for a humanity liberated from the terror of death and eternal punishment.

But his dreams had failed to come true. Life had

continued with its mask of ugliness and disillusion. And then even the dream was prohibited. The catastrophe came crashing down like an earthquake overturning the face of the earth, revealing ghastly abysses, devastated landscapes, inhospitable spaces, wart-afflicted faces, and comatose bodies.

Boualem Yekker remembers the demonstrations of force: detachments of bearded men marching in tight ranks, their eyes rolled upward, with the ecstatic look of the enlightened. They would shout their determination to purify society in order to bring it in line with the commandments of the Almighty. The men they brought to power were their replicas in every aspect: the same sense of certainty, the same contempt for dialogue (from the moment they possess the Truth!), and the same inflexibility in their decisions. The people who were expecting the new masters to show themselves to be more concerned than their predecessors with finding them work, housing, and a more compassionate daily existence were rapidly brought down to earth. The first obsessions of the leaders, in a hurry to realize God's will on earth, were forbidding alcohol, fighting coeducation, separating men and women in the workplace, and closing a great many classy hotels, accused of promoting debauchery.

Some men, citing divine will and legitimacy, decided to shape the world in the image of their dream and their madness. Many citizens discovered that God could reveal a grisly face.

The result is there under one's eyes: couples coerced, hitched up under the same yoke in order to perpetuate and multiply the precious species of believers. Women reduce their presence to a nameless and faceless black shadow. They hug the walls, humble and submissive, almost apologizing for having been born. Men walk two or three meters ahead of their wives; every now and then they cast a look backwards to make sure their property is still there; they are embarrassed, not to say exasperated, by this presence that is both undesirable and necessary.

The future is a closed door

. . . As for Karl Marx, the German Jew, the essence of his the-ory rests on the double affirmation that God does not exist and that life is matter. This doctrine, quite obviously, is one of those we will fight and—with God's help!—we will destroy.

Boualem Yekker slowly and wearily puts the phi-losophy book back down. These are the kinds of things they are teaching his daughter in the new uni-versity textbooks, developed since theologians have come to lead the country. Philosophy, that austere but beautiful window open to questioning and doubt, has closed on certainties and ostracism.

Bitterly, Boualem again sees the result of this brain-washing (which furthermore is not afraid of having recourse to physical methods: recalcitrant students and teachers have been molested on many occasions). He sees Kenza again, an Electra dressed in black, a close-minded and fierce virgin, cloaked in morality and anathemas.

A few days before she left, she had flung at him that she was ashamed of such a father, deaf to the voice of God, excluded from the clemency of the Last Judgment and the rapture of the Resurrection. It was the hour of prayer. When the muezzin had sent forth his call in a triumphant voice, infinitely amplified by microphones shaking with decibels, three prayer mats had appeared simultaneously— "miraculous flying carpets," Boualem thought—and wife, daughter, and son were lost in poses of prayer. When they stood up again from their devotions, the daughter angrily picked up her mat and, turning to her father, let out a flood of abuses.

A statue raised up as the righter of wrongs. An implacable virago, abandoned by any femininity. The illness of fanaticism had attacked her. Her super-human, inhuman faith had shattered all attachments in her woven by flesh and affection. The loving little girl, who had always felt very close to her father, had died. It was as if the young girl, now covered with su-perior certainties, had discarded a cocoon and had been granted a new armor without any groove what-ever for tenderness, weakness, and the equivocations of the nonbeliever.

The daughter was trembling while spawning her

criticism. She was in a state of exaltation, working herself up, like someone who, having crossed a long-
dreaded frontier, wants to go to the very end of the
challenge to ward off some demon.

Boualem had kept silent. He had found nothing
to reply to the violent indictment. He was not angry.
He, too, had arrived at a limit beyond which meaning, feelings, and conventions are decentralized,
abolished. Or maybe he did not want to speak in
order to keep his suffering intact, for words appease
and exorcise. Boualem did not lose his calm; he even
had the presence of mind to realize that he could
consider himself lucky in view of the lot of others. In
fact, an unhappy neighbor, having come home in a
state of drunkenness a few days before, had his jaw
broken by his son, newly converted to the party of
God's representatives on earth.

Now, as he keeps an eye on the book dedicated to
the new kind of philosophy, Boualem is thinking of a
little girl, a small human being of intelligence, intensity, mischievousness, and love. He had known a girl
like that, had fused with her, for she was a scion of his
flesh. He was never able to convince himself of the actual existence of a barbarian tradition of the ancient
Arabs, although it was reported in many writings: the

burial of little girls, still alive, among warrior tribes for whom only boys counted. Is there anything more beautiful on earth than a little girl? Can a man exist with a heart capable of committing the horrors thus told?

A few images, both sweet and overwhelming, a few helpful and painful feelings torment him, trying to make their way toward seizing the whole of memory's space. For men like Boualem gaze exclusively toward memory. With the future crossed out, the past has become an obsession. It is an uncontrollable flood that no dike can manage to keep back. It is like a Garden of Eden that radiates through the darkness. At night, it keeps its disciples awake, like an agonizing pain. A pain from which you cannot escape even by finding refuge in the future, for the future is a closed door.

His wounded memory, crushed beneath the millstone of time, drowned in a horizon whirling around like a stormy sea, stops on the image of an alert and mischievous little girl. It is fall, with trees growing cold and leaves beginning to turn red. Nature is resting after having turned verdant and frolicked in the spring, shimmered with its hues of gold and glitter in the summer. Now there are shades of sweetness, nonchalance, and reconciliation. Nature is like a mature woman who still has some charms but has quieted down, has put aside her vanity, her makeup, and her seductiveness.

In the middle of this soothing nature where no violence glares, a little girl is gamboling in the dead leaves. She is gathering pine cones that the wind has shaken loose. She bends down, stands up, and starts off on a little run before bending down again. Sometimes, as she approaches, a bird surfaces from the grass and, zigzagging in its flight, goes off to sit down a bit farther away or to hide in the foliage of a tree. Little elf ordering the elements by waving her arm in the air, Kenza struggles against the wind, her inquisitive face forward, her brown curls fighting. An innocent creature, full of enthusiasm, curiosity, and questions, Kenza is exploring the mysteries of the world, decoding the murmurs of the earth with the magic wand of her entrenched candor. The hypocritical and reproachful look of the Universal Moralizer cannot reach her; it slips on her innocent and rebellious flesh like the drool of a toad on a waterlily. Suddenly, in her race after pine cones and her pursuit of birds, Kenza hits an obstacle, falls, and begins to let out piercing cries. Boualem, who comes running at high speed, has a moment of panic: a short spike coming out of the soil has injured the child, putting a deep gash in her calf. As he rushes to his car with Kenza howling in his arms, Boualem thinks suddenly that, if his daughter should die, he would never want another child—out of devotion to her memory. He even wonders whether he could survive her, for going on living would in itself constitute a betrayal.

Evening has fallen now. With the semidarkness and the furtive shadows in which everything merges, the noble and the contemptible, the generous and the sordid, with the semidarkness favorable to spying and conspiracy, Boualem feels a desire for physical vengeance. If the system, the ideas, and the men who have made his daughter into what she is today were to come and be materialized in one person, what would he not be capable of making that one endure! Could all the humiliations and suffering he has been subjected to, all the violence that has come out of it, be mastered? For a short while now, Boualem has been convinced that he is capable of violence. Secretly, he is even preparing for it, for he knows that one day he will be forced to use it. In his mind, killing has almost become a symbolic and conciliatory act, a simple rite of exorcism whereby violence and blood come close to being purely abstract.

He also knows that there are thousands like him. But mistrust is everywhere. How can those who want to fight meet when mistrust has been raised to the level of neurosis? You are afraid to reveal yourself to your neighbor, but also to your friend, your brother, and your offspring. Everyone is barricaded behind a bulwark of hypocrisy and artificial piety. When you are not sure of the reliability of the terrain, silence is the best complement to this armor. For the least little crack that shows, the least bit of a lowered defense can prove fatal. And the massive club of the Regulators of the Faith will then come and crush you like an ordinary dung fly who has the gall to settle on a cake.

The message suppressed

This is the letter he has written to his daughter but which he will never send her.

I shall come home from traveling
and shall find you asleep.
The racket of the furniture will have fallen silent,
animals will have softly disappeared,
and all the drums of the house
will have once again become living but discreet
*   skins.*

I always arrive in the true deferment
of pulsations,
when lime, clay, and their whiteness
have occupied everything once more.

I arrive
and gradually see emergence:

first you, orchestrating colors and movements,
giving the animals their clamor back,
directing perilous flights.
Then the objects,
proud of their prowess,
unleash the ebullience of the merry-go-round.

You will look for the acrobatic dogs
of the dream
between the astonished sheets,
you will shake the shimmers of light one by one,
and life will settle down again.

You wake up
And the house becomes a carnival.

For that we will live,
for that we will die . . .

Boualem remembers the beginning, the source, the torrent that was going to carry everything away:

It is like a dike breaking. The gesticulating and shouting tide, vomited out by the adjoining streets, pours out onto the square that fills up in the twinkling of an eye. The circles of the first arrivals grow tighter and tighter until they form only one compact mass whose density increases as the tributaries meet.

The gigantic crowd begins to turn in place, to squirm, like lava hitting an obstacle that is too high and surging backwards in waves. A cry is heard, as if coming from one colossal lung that is the totality of the thousands of lungs, a cry that rips the zenith and rises to the sky: "God is the greatest!" It is an irrepressible delirium carried forward from gullet to gullet. Then follow deep, amplified sighs, signs of mortification or ecstasy that fall back to earth like exhalations of the Apocalypse. Ecstasy floats in the air, impregnates every puff of air they breathe. The squeezing human mass, swaying like the multicolored dragons in Chinese carnivals, possesses one single enormous heart, galvanized and immersed in the brazier of faith. The collective sigh that ends every incantation is like a seismic rumble cracking the entrails of the world.

The gathering takes on aspects of the Last Judgment. The world will have to answer for itself, humanity is going to appear at the sentencing with its beauties and its depravities. Nothing will be forgotten, nothing will be forgiven.

The spiritual guide of this crowd, a young man with olive skin and a thin beard, climbs up onto the pedestal of the monument adorning the square and immediately renewed shouts rise up: "God is the greatest!"

But the orator has barely to raise his arm for a deadly silence to fall. The man with the thin beard speaks excitedly in a lashing voice that rises or falls depending on the intensity of the inner fire feeding him. Then the voice grows hoarse, becomes wrenching, and the words coming out of his mouth resemble sobs.

The crowd in ferment picks up on his words:
"For that we will live,
for that we will die . . . "
The orator remains as if deferential and then begins a

verse the rioters rhythmically chant along with him. Finally, he comes down from the pedestal and is lost in the crush. The crowd is feverish and agitated, shock waves running through it. Then, like a ball being divided, the impenetrable mass produces a line that stretches out and whose head ends up being lost from sight. The recent orator, the man of contagious exaltation, is the end of the line: he is the finger dividing the human spool. The crowd has appropriated a sloping street leading to the shantytown. At the head of the march, incantations and slogans are launched, traveling through the long procession and then dying out, replaced by other incantations and other slogans. The words are punctuated by deep sighs delving intensely into chests that ache with all the world's injustices.

The group stops many times in front of homes or balconies from which the curious are watching. In a voice that mixes entreaties with threats, the marchers urge the men to come out and join them. The curious, both stimulated and terrorized by this human force advancing like an inexorable flood, often come down to mix in with the crowd and are immediately won over by the fervent madness. They, too, pick up the slogans with bulging eyes and loudly shouting voices, submerged in a trance. They are paralyzed by the collective rapture that dispossesses them of themselves, makes them into fleshless shadows moved about by irresistible springs.

The crowd comes hurtling down the sloping street, floods the city's space, goes around the blocks of houses, engulfing the more modest obstacles. There is no force that can stop it: there is no police officer in sight; one would almost say the country has no core of authority, no agent ranked high enough to maintain order and clear the streets.

Therapists of the spirit

The preachers and the new candidates had started by ridiculing all allegedly rational knowledge, all currents of thought that had dared to place mankind in the center of their focus, thereby forgetting that Adam's son is but a malleable figure, a simple wisp of straw in the hands of the Almighty! Darwin, Mendeleyev, and Omar Khayyam were their favorite victims; they were a permanent object of jokes, malevolence, and sarcasm.

Strange pontiffs, wearing turbans, their eyes outlined in kohl and their beards dyed with henna, proclaimed themselves to be scholars and appropriated the last word in fields as varied as nuclear physics, cybernetics, astronomy, bureaucracy, linguistics, and psychoanalysis. Jung, Paul Dirac, Arthur Stanley Eddington, Mohammed Iqbal, Lord Rutherford, Gandhi, Marcuse, and Lévi-Strauss were judged, demystified, downgraded, ridiculed, and swept aside in short television broadcasts. Such programs usually end with a resounding burst of laughter by the turbaned expert, who waves universal destitution away with the back of his hand and swells with conceit over having put things in their place, reestablished humility and the relativity of knowledge, and toppled statues of overrated proportions.

The new approved knowledge contains three basic rules:

1. Science has the right to pay attention only to those questions not settled in the Book.

2. Any scientific result and any scientific discovery must be challenged by the Text in order to find justification for them there.

3. Our religion is the source of all knowledge: any scientific or moral law, any legislation decreed in the time preceding this religion, when humanity was steeped in darkness, lies, and barbarism, is null and void.

Mosques, universities, the radio, television, and even the athletic clubs were recruited to spread the new scholarship. Television, in particular, saw itself assigned with a first-class role. Three-quarters of its programs consist of skillful sermon-courses and documentaries of a special kind, in which incantations mix with pseudoscientific arguments, and where verses of the Book are mixed with chemical formulas and equations. An astronomy club was assigned the task of reconciling the solar system's nine planets and the mysteries of the Andromeda galaxy with "the seven heavens and the earth" of the Book. Innumerable associations—among which the Feminine League for the Commitment to the Path of God, the League for Social and Cultural Reform, the Religious League of the Plastic Arts, the National Association of Pious Literature, and the Theological Association for Civilizing Edification—took control over society, conducting a project of consciousness raising, but also of surveillance, harassment, establishing files, and censure.

It is at the instigation of these associations that collections are held to cover the costs of publishing the books disseminating the new scholarship, that advocacy groups are organized in public squares, that punitive expeditions are initiated against places of entertainment such as theaters and casinos, as well as against individuals whose ideas or behavior are considered to be reprehensible.

Inside these associations women are very active.

As it is easier for them than for men to enter homes, it is through them that a department of information could be set up and that entire districts have been carefully registered and classified along with their ways and customs, lifestyle, political coloring, level of devotion, and the moral ideas of each inhabitant. These women also taught housewives and mothers to control their husbands' peccadilloes, to raise their children in the path of God and the rejection of any knowledge inspired by the advocates of sacrilege and immorality, to fight against a godless society that clever managers of Satan attempt to implant on earth, and to resist the so-called science that strips the world of its faith. They called themselves "therapists of the spirit."

Weather forecasts have been banned from television and no newspaper is authorized to publish them. Already during the previous regime the forecast was presented with profuse expressions of "if God wills it so," "according to the will of the Almighty," "if the All-Powerful who commands the clouds does not decide otherwise." Henceforth, however, the forecast is quite simply suppressed, for how can one argue and quibble over patterns known only to God?

Starting at the hour of the former weather fore-cast, two new television broadcasts enjoy special attention, maintained by spots that return every hour. Broadcast daily right after the news, during prime time, their titles are "Light on Light" and "Irrefutable Grandeur." Based on documentary films showing scenes of animal life, landscapes, and scientific achievements, both broadcasts celebrate the omnipotence of God, creator of all wonders and director of all laws and all balances. There is no attempt at scientific explanation at all, no rational look at things, no questions delineated. Each law, each detail, each form of natural harmony is perceived as a minuscule facet of the blinding mirror in which the light of the Revelation is reflected. Glory to the infinite, to God, the master of dawns and dusks, the generator of all phenomena, the One who creates the elements, embellishes them, commands them, makes them move and stay in place!

In these emphatic and farcical broadcasts, a short, sarcastic, and condescending remark is addressed to some biologist, geneticist, or astronomer claiming to encompass the mysterious power of the Creator in a few formulas. The cathodic eye is all-powerful; not only does it extract the only knowledge that is reasonable, but it also scrutinizes us to see if the virus of doubt has begun to nestle in among some of us. Glory and submission to God, glory to His creations without number that no book is capable of evaluating, questioning, or decoding!

Future generations will not even be able to immerse themselves in the anxiety and impertinence of books, for books will have been burned—to make place for the one, the irremovable Book of resigned certainty.

One should come
from nowhere

Some snapshots and attitudes stolen from time,
which is merciless, a few images withdrawn from the
wheel that knows no respite and, in passing and passing by again, crushes and disfigures. Boualem Yekker
is looking at photos, traces left by those who are
absent. These are the images that stopped time, that
prevent him from being a man without a memory.
That allow him to resist becoming what they want to
make him into: a wreck; a tree stump, its roots sev-
ered, its sap dry.

The new order would like to prune humanity, but
also every individual human being. Expurgate, am-
putate, purify. Of memory leave only what celebrates
the Revelation, of knowledge leave only what asks no
questions, of man leave only the part that is submissive to God—a God whose outlines have been carefully drawn by the new masters: He knows no love, no

forgiveness, no compassion, and no tolerance. He is the God of vengeance and punishment.

The hinterland of memory, with its rebellious songs, its living sources, its easygoing gods, its protecting trees, its harsh or fertile stretches, its people made of love and conflicts—the hinterland has been erased, swallowed up in the gaping hole of devouring faith. To be a member of the herd of acquiescent believers, of the herd of slaves shackled to the Word of Truth that does not even have a former dream of freedom in its memory, one should come from nowhere. One should be a mere graft that can be sliced off at any time. For the ax of faith makes no compromises, does not tremble or hesitate for one moment.

What this ax would like to cut off first is the path leading to the child, the umbilical cord that serves as an Ariadne's thread. The little Boualem, stuffed with dreams, with unbridled desires and unlimited horizons, must disappear to make room for the man controlled by piety's bit, fettered by the millstone of the Truth revealed. A man chased away from his earlier territories, from land full of game where unexpected animals cavorted. A man whose roots have been cut off, without a childhood and without a paradise to look for: there is no more Eden behind, there is only one paradise ahead, promised to those who redouble their prayers, their zeal, and their sacrifices on the path to the All-Powerful.

Boualem is summoned to renounce his hidden treasures, to abandon his secrets and his wounds, his exuberant joys and his tears. He must give up everything: homes he has lived in; heartbreaking farewells; foggy dawns when the way to school seemed like an adventure; walks in the fields looking for wild fruits and birds' nests; the panting sea burned by the setting sun; landscapes undressed and bruised by winter; books read with a lump in your throat, a swollen chest, a palpitating heart; different kinds of music that envelop you, fill your head with song, and send you up to the stars.

To find access to the path of God, you must become an orphan from all that. Stop up your ears, tame your eyes, rein in the thrusts of your heart, tear up your books that are too bold, and break everything that vibrates and sings. You must become an orphan, stripped of all belongings. Rid yourself of your carnal father. Separate yourself from your mother, not only from her flesh but also from the memory of her tenderness.

101

Boualem has not thought of his parents in a very long time. The memory he has of them is one of the most unpleasant, and he feels absolutely no need to exhume and revive it. He has thrown everything relating to his parents into a well of oblivion in which he has also flung his quite joyless childhood and the places that gave him shelter—all of it in one neatly tied-up bundle, with a stone attached to it so it would never surface again. He has often been horrified at the thought that perhaps his children might act the same way regarding him, burying the memory of him in some dark and repulsive place that no one would even want to come near.

The father had died first, at an age barely greater than Boualem's present age. A shadow, both furtive and burdensome, that left very few traces on his son—just some stripes in his memory, similar to the scars of wounds. A haughty and taciturn man. Kept his words to a minimum. Rapacious as a usurer: "Don't you hear what's being said to you?" "Aren't you ready yet?" "Not happy with the food?" He wouldn't even look at you when he spoke. Why did he have a falling-out with words? He must have spoken such a harsh language inside himself that it would have ripped his throat apart had it come out.

The mother, tiny and cantankerous, was more imposing; she was invasive to the point of engulfing and crushing you. She saw all her relationships with others in terms of domination. Boualem had often thought that she had had children without any love at all, but merely to have people available to serve her. Toward the end of her life, she had become unbearable, and Boualem couldn't wait to see her leave forever a house she had made unlivable.

Boualem wonders if today his children don't have even more hostile feelings toward him—no doubt a great deal of contempt in addition to the hatred itself.

He is looking at the photos. They have a special value, for perhaps he will never have any others showing these people. Human beings gone forever, no doubt, but not carried off by the illnesses of poverty and old age like his father and mother; they expired in their prime without having had time to become heavy, undesirable, or disfigured by infirmity. Somewhere deep inside, he knows those faces will never be found again; he has gained enough courage now not to deny reality.

He looks at the portraits. Already separated. Each enclosed in its own frame. Not a single group picture showing a family happy to be reunited. Aside from these photographs, there will soon be no more than a few episodes in Boualem's memory and he will not even know whether they are dreams or actual memories.

The portrait that moves him most is the one of Kenza when she was four or five years old (he is too depressed to get up and check each dated picture). An independent and frail human being, a little woman both determined and subdued, with a strangely hard look, as if deciding to confront the incongruities of the world without blinking. Her plump lips are tightly closed, but one wonders whether she is not suppressing a barely controlled laugh. A child's face—already indecipherable. A face hesitating between pouting and laughter, between naughtiness and solemnity. The little body moving forward into life, on her guard, already beginning to question the world, to observe it, size it up, defy it, and sound it out to detect its traps and its vast beaches of happiness. The whole meaning, the whole weight, the whole joy, and the whole pain of the world lie in that face, which should be carefree but is already watchful like a small stalked animal.

Boualem knows he must give up on these faces.

That is perhaps the only way for him to set his grief free, to let it go away, be dissolved so that he himself can find some meaning in what surrounds him, in what continues to supplement him, in what life remains to him.

He would like to be sleeping—to sink into a deep sleep, like the final one from which one does not emerge. He has been having sleepless nights for so long, his consciousness in a state of alert, refusing to be distracted by a moment of rest. Sometimes he finds himself in a kind of antechamber of respite, hesitating between the threshold of annihilation and that of a painful vigil; but he almost always gets caught in the second room.

He no longer dares to sleep in the bed where he used to sleep with his wife. At first he had opted for the living-room sofa but, since it is very uncomfortable, he put down a single mattress next to it. There he camps out, waiting to depart for a more hospitable place and time.

The unknown arbiter

The envelope has neither stamp nor seal; it has not been sent through the mail.

For months now, Boualem Yekker has been opening his mailbox with a great deal of apprehension; every time he hopes to find it empty. He is not expecting any message of concern, love, or hope. Times no longer allow for such consideration. The present situation reminds him of his adolescence, during the war, when you would dread any kind of note, for it was almost always a summons or other libel that boded nothing good.

His hand trembles a little as he reaches for the envelope. His name is outlined in an impressive handwriting with lengthening and curved letters. He hesitates a moment before opening it but, once he decides to, he tears it open feverishly, as if in a hurry to assure himself that it does not contain his death warrant.

The sheet of graph paper opens with the sacramental formula glorifying the Merciful One. Then follows a terse message:

Given your culture and your knowledge (making the error of your ways unpardonable), the society of heathens will welcome you with open arms for services rendered. It needs men like you to spread its immorality and its abject plans. But you are being offered a last way out. Do not be the unconscious instrument of a diabolical project. Rather, put your knowledge and the days remaining to you (life on earth is not eternal) in the service of the highest morality.

From someone who, without too many illusions, only hopes to be the cause of your awakening, for the Master of Creation, Who has restricted himself from doing evil, leads astray whom He wants and guides whom He wants toward the straight and narrow path.

Boualem's anxiety diminishes as he continues reading. All things considered, the message he had feared so much is mild. It could even be seen as benevolent compared to some of the messages that are circulating—injunctions, denunciations, and other death threats. One of the most revolting methods consists of sending a shroud to the designated victim. It seems that the mere sight of this object brings on an extreme state of shock in the addressee. The good soul who has directed himself to Boualem belongs to the school of charitable missionaries, one of the rare men in this country for whom death has not become the only argument and the only point of reference.

Boualem stuffs the letter into his pocket before going inside. For a while now he has been feeling the apprehensions of a fanatic. He methodically inspects his tiny bit of garden and even the inside of his house. He checks and rechecks doors and windows to make certain they are locked. The least little sound he hears (or imagines?) impels him to be on his guard, sometimes even pulling him out of bed, ready to hide or fight. He lives the way a hunted animal does.

The message he has received this day constitutes a kind of happy ending to these long moments of anguish. So that's really all they want from me, Boualem says to himself; they want to bring me back to the straight and narrow. What good souls, so attentive to the lot of their fellow man! A strange and unlivable planet. Opposite this world, this logic that causes blood to flow out of passion, that has claimed the right to destroy people in order to save their souls, there is the other world with an equally implacable

109

logic, but a cold one, killing with algorithms, the binary system, and persnickety computer science. The world split in two: murderous exaltation against all-consuming algebra.

Inside the house, Boualem drops into his easy chair with a sigh of relief. He hasn't even gone on his usual inspection meant to expose the prowler who has come to eliminate him. The message he just received has reassured him, made it known to him that there are tender hearts among the arbiters swarming through the city, who alert you, who appeal to your wisdom before the ax comes down on you. He would like to be listening to some beautiful music, languorous and restful. He thinks of Faïrouz. Every time he feels the need to be reconciled with the Arabs, he plays a cassette by Faïrouz. But he doesn't have the energy to get out of his chair and put a cassette into the machine. He is dozing deliciously in the depths of the leatherette. Will sleep, which he has so often coveted, be joining him today?

The shrill ring of the telephone breaks the silence. Boualem jumps but doesn't have the courage to get up. His legs feel like cotton, stiff. The distance between his body and the phone seems insurmountable, a vast swampy terrain, a desert of sharp stones. In the hope the ringing will stop, he waits, trying to control his nervousness.

Finally he gets up and, his heart pounding, goes toward the stubborn ringing. He picks up the phone. The voice on the other end of the line says in a funereal tone:

"You are a dead man. Prepare yourself to suffer the wrath of your Creator."

And the strange caller hangs up. Now Boualem is shaking with rage. He wants his persecutor to call back so he can heap abuses on him, pour all the anger he has been swallowing for months out over him, all the rebellion brewing inside him for which there is no outlet. He remains standing next to the phone, waiting for it to ring again. In his head he is preparing a fine chain of insults and challenges for this cowardly maniac. For once, he congratulates himself on being alone: neither his wife nor his children will have to hear the series of curses, invectives, and scathing words that are to follow. All the expressions of indignation that his sense of civic responsibility has been suppressing for ages in the deep darkness of his throat are going to make use of the wide-open door of his lips today. Finally Boualem

111

will be delivered from an anger that has been hibernating inside him for half a century.

He waits for the phone to ring, as if for a message of love. Realizing it is a losing battle, he goes and sits back down in his chair. Then, feverishly, he gets up to prepare a haphazard dinner: fried eggs and peppers. Sitting at the table, he stares in a stupor, all his hunger gone, at the two huge yellow eyes locked inside the gelatin of white. He has no mouth, no stomach any longer. He is nothing but a mass of nerves, a ball being tightened until the thread breaks. A warning is unleashed inside him, obliterating the usual needs of the body.

Returning to his chair, he sits down and—delicious sensation—starts to doze off, to slowly detach himself from the oppressive atmosphere, and to float, his body and conscience ethereal, relieved of the suffering and blackness each new day hauls in.

Heavy with sleep, he moves from the chair to his mattress on the floor. This night will not be like the others; its intensity will make it a night to remember. Boualem feels he is inside the skin of a romantic young man who hears the night breathe, who lets himself be rocked by the sound of the wind and the chorus of the rain. He is in harmony with the world and at peace with his body. He is floating on a veil of gauze, subtly undulating to better couple with his contortions and absorb his sudden movements. Healing cotton wool surrounds him; he rolls around voluptuously in recesses and fleecy clouds, sometimes almost suffocating and opening his mouth wide. Blessed night of all nights! In complicity, Boualem's body and spirit are setting sail toward the desired region, the earthly Eden of sleep . . .

This time, the ringing freezes him. Boualem starts violently, cold sweat rushing over his body. His heart begins to beat so wildly that he starts to choke: a gigantic inner organ seems squeezed inside his chest, obstructing his breathing. What savage ringing is this? What world, what century does it come from? From what monster does it emanate? Boualem has been swimming in a universe of opalescent, evanescent substances, of sensual sinusoids. And suddenly an implacable instrument, shrieking from its metal mouth, brutally evicts him.

Boualem begins to tremble, as if he had been dunked into a basin of ice water. He tries to pull his legs up to his belly, tries to curl inward to form a ball resistant enough to protest the noise and the cold that the metal voice is spilling all around. But he cannot move; his body is in shock, frozen by the acrimonious tongue in its aggressive pitch. He lets the ringing reverberate, lashing him with blows that come in rapid succession. He holds his breath for fear that the persecutor on the other end of the line might realize he is there.

The phone finally stops ringing, but Boualem is too nervous to regain the state of grace that might usher him back into sleep. He stays in a fetal position, shivering beneath the blankets, unable even to decide whether to get up and go to the toilet, though his sudden need to urinate is urgent.

Convinced that the light will deliver him from this nightmare, Boualem waits impatiently for the day to appear. He wants to know how much longer he has to wait. Unable to resist the need to look at his watch, he gets up and turns on the light. It is 3:50 A.M. He walks into the bathroom and empties his bladder.

Rolled up in his blankets once more, he closes his eyes and forces himself to think of soothing landscapes that might carry him off to sleep. When at last his nervousness leaves him, he sinks into a state of torpor, losing all sense of time.

Cars begin to move around. Sporadic at first, the

rhythm soon picks up. Roosters join in. Then, all of a sudden, as if a lock had been opened, daylight floods in, restoring familiar faces to objects and spaces.

On this day, a day of exceptional flavor and color, Boualem takes time with his coffeemaking. It is both a day of celebration and a day of farewell. To have escaped from so unpropitious a night—one of the most painful he has ever spent! In some way, that night has matured him; now, as he approaches the half-century mark, he seems to have discovered the essence of things: he senses that he will now be able to make certain decisions accordingly, real decisions that will not stem from dreams or from a flight forward. In the darkness and the cold of solitude in which no presence whatever could distract or assist him, he has, for the first time, gropingly touched the ghastly face of reality. Henceforth he will fear it no more; he will look it straight in the eye.

He feels like taking stock, making an account of things objectively and without panic. For one thing, he knows without fail—and he will never again be deluded—that he belongs to a marginal and hounded species that will not be long in disappearing. Never again will he be able, at the top of his voice and with transported heart, to launch into the tough and

115

confident song of the community, the song that brings rest to the soul and reconciles one with crude reality. This community is his no longer: it rejects him, and he no longer cares for it. An almost amiable divorce. If it were not for the threats and the bullying that make his life impossible, they—his society and he—could have lived side by side, their backs turned to each other, without asking anything from each other.

He slowly savors his coffee, elated, like a lover waiting for the hour of rendezvous.

At last he leaves to go to the bookstore. As he opens his gate, a group of children who seem to be lying in ambush disperse. Boualem catches only snatches of their murmurings. As he passes a few meters beyond them, he hears the sardonic sentence flung at his back, a challenge soon picked up by several voices:

"On the day of the Last Judgment, He will have heathens grow donkey's ears."

Boualem hurries on, but the phrase pursues him, carried now by stronger voices, voices that become more and more menacing.

Born to have a body

The bookstore has been closed.

The committee for the preservation of collective morality has decided to allocate the space to a use that is both more profitable and more honorable—but that, for the moment, it does not specify.

Boualem Yekker was not notified. One morning, when he went to the bookstore as usual, he found that the lock had been changed and a sign had been attached to the door. The sign stipulated that the sovereign Community had decided to reclaim a possession that belongs first to God and then to the Community. As for the merchandise in the place, its owner would be alerted in due time if he would be expected to retrieve it.

Boualem stands in front of the door, stunned. Should he try to enter his bookstore or turn back? He stands there, perplexed, incapacitated, and sheepish, not knowing what to do with his arms and legs, as if the first had forgotten how to act and the second did not know how to take him away from there. Suddenly there is revelation. An unusual peace comes over him. Only a few minutes ago he was dazed, and now he feels delivered—the incomprehensible deliverance that sometimes comes with total defeat.

Being separated from books is the greatest upheaval he has faced in his life—even the departure of his family does not represent as profound a break with his past and as obvious a confiscation of his future. It is as if a black wall had been erected. A wall all around him, preventing him from looking either ahead or behind.

Boualem suddenly thinks of those distant relatives he would occasionally see in the country and who didn't have a single book in their home. Every time he visited, he used to wonder how those people could live, without the smell of paper, without turning pages in which metaphors, ideas, and adventures were rustling. Perhaps now, in the time remaining to him, he himself will be living the life of those people, knowing horizons such as theirs. For who is to say that, after closing the bookstore, the Vigilant Brothers will not burst into his house to root out every last book he owns? Until now, nothing has been able to stop the exorcist madness of these crazed redeemers. They have decided to polish the sky so that their faith might be reflected there. They want to begin by washing away the unseemly clouds made up of books.

Books have been the compost in which Boualem's life ripened, to the point where his bookish hands and his carnal hands, his paper body and his body of flesh and blood very often overlap and mingle. Boualem himself no longer sees a clear distinction. He has met so many characters in books, he has come into contact with so many unforgettable destinies that his own life would be nothing without them. It was a little through contact with life and a great deal through contact with books that ideas germinated in him, that ideals took root, that voluptuous feelings and waves of pleasure or anger ran through his trembling body, leaving lasting traces behind. It has happened to him, as to any persevering reader, that he could speak informally with the most prestigious characters, penetrate their intimacy, read their emotions and their thoughts as if through a glass door. From the very start, he had a particular affection for unhappy, tormented, and problematical authors: he preferred Du Bellay to Ronsard, Ben Jonson to Shakespeare, Keats to Lord Byron, Rousseau to Voltaire, Dostoyevsky to Tolstoy, Alfred de Vigny to Victor Hugo, and Hafiz Ibrahim to Ahmad Chawqi. He stayed with the classics. Contemporary literature puzzles him with its frivolity or with its formal, abstruse games in which the human soul finds itself on the scrap heap, and where mankind's destiny is played like a computer program with multiple entries.

He remembers an episode in his life when, barely out of childhood, his cousin and he, having just entered middle school, were on the beach having a conversation about Voltaire and Rousseau. His cousin was defending the superiority of Voltaire while Boualem was giving his vote to Rousseau. The discussion grew animated, and suddenly his cousin looked him up and down, then gazed at the horizon and solemnly stated:

"But Voltaire has more talent."

A decisive and murderous argument: Boualem remained silent. He sheepishly lowered his head: he didn't know what the word *talent* meant.

Soon after this incident, his big brother brought home a monumental book: *History of Aviation* by

René Chambe of the French Academy. It was one of the most beautiful windows that opened for Boualem onto the world of exploits and adventures. The whole sky suddenly came tumbling down to him, became a meadow for his wildest dreams to frolic in. He grew familiar down to the smallest details with the impatience, the joy, the exploits, and the misadventures of Clément Ader, Santos-Dumont, Latham, the Wright brothers, Guillaumet, Hélène Boucher, and Mermoz. He knew Lindbergh's crossing hour by hour, as he knew the dramatic failure of Nungesser and Coli. The adventure of Aéropostale, the flight over the cordilleras, mechanical breakdowns in the desert, ocean crossings were his own ports of call and his own feats. Later on, when television became a gadget every household possessed, he didn't miss one series on Blériot, not one documentary on Guynemer. For a long time he lived in the wide-open sky, undulating by proxy, shaken in his cabin by the emotions of the adventure in which death circled around like a bird of prey.

And no one need think he had not enjoyed a real youth, a youth outside of books. He, too, had been part of those multitudes of people who know they were born to have a body. The cadences of

childhood wonder, the turmoil of adolescent passions and dreams had vibrated within him like tight
strings. Before becoming waves of memory, floods
had surged through him, sensual and insistent to the
point of suffering and obsession.

The house he lived in then had few of the comforts of the one he lives in today, which even has the
luxury of a sickly lemon tree, an unexpected oasis for
birds impeded by cement who come to seek refuge
there, to rest, chirp, and even frisk about before continuing on their way to some verdant Eden. His
earlier house had been oppressive. It was located
in a tightly packed quarter of the city, where the
sun wouldn't enter and birds wouldn't venture.
Boualem had hardly any of the toys he saw in the
hands of other children and that he dreamed of
owning: a horse on wheels, chubby and round-
bottomed rubber people and animals; for a long
time he had yearned for an air gun.

But a ball was within his reach. The children of
the neighborhood had appropriated a vacant lot
about two kilometers away. Their soccer matches did
not follow regulation time but lasted a whole afternoon, until night fell and the ball started to hide
even from their sharp vision. Sometimes—marvelous

moments—girls would stop to watch. Then the players would lose their heads, outdo each other, in-
crease their efforts and irregularities, and become
ridiculous. Fortunately, the referee did not excel
where strictness and punctuality were concerned!
When he, too, was overcome by the desire to show
the girls that he was the absolute master of this
battlefield the match would end in blood.

Boualem had a friend, a real dullard, completely
intoxicated with soccer, who eventually became a
professional player. At the time, he used to tell
Boualem grandiloquent stories whose heroes were
soccer players—goalkeepers usually. One of these
stories told of the heroic goalie of a minor-league
team. He refused to be part of a scheme the managers had planned whereby his team was to lose.
Once in front of his goal and in a fit of honor, he did
his utmost, to the point where he ended up having
twenty players against him on the field. Resisting
until the end, when the game was over, he was
beaten to death by his teammates and their oppo-
nents, who had joined forces. Another story told of
the tragic ending of an obviously extraordinary goal-
keeper. Exasperated by the panache of this goalie
whose cage remained as intact as a virgin's hymen,

his adversaries slipped a knife inside the ball. The moment the valiant athlete dove and stopped the ball beneath him, the knife penetrated his heart . . .

The other solution for the life and insatiable desires of aroused bodies was the sea—its deep and pearly belly, its breathlessness like that of a tired woman after lovemaking, its lazy stretches. Sometimes, tiny wavelets would run across its infinite space, gooseflesh dotting its chilled animal's back. There, too, other friendships were formed, for they gathered there in groups. Other fables and myths were born there, whose heroes were not goalies but naked young girls, or else phenomenal fish that would divert the fishermen. Seasoned by the sea breeze, a whiff of iodine and brine, these stories would kindle the desire coiled in adolescent loins like a reptile pounded by the sun and aerated by gentle gusts of wind.

A girls' high school stood on the road to the beach. Both coming and going, when they were returning home before nightfall, the boys would stop a few meters from the gate. Communicating with the girls was very difficult, but silent love affairs and imaginary adventures would sprout, blossom, and intensify to inhabit the days and nights of the boys (and, who knows, of the girls too, perhaps?), who let themselves be taken in by their own game and their fantasies, embroiled in illusion and swagger.

Even impoverished youth could counter misery with vigor, beauty, the impertinence of one's body, and the boldness of one's desire. Youth clinging to life, irrigated by the sun like an invincible fire! On prosperous days, you could sit down on a terrace and buy yourself a drink or a bitter and delicious beer. Those were titillating moments when life would change colors, when your head sang out and would sink into a dizzying celebration. With little sips, the light outside would penetrate the body, radiating and burning like a torch in the night.

How times have changed since then! You would think you were in another country, not to say on another planet. Today's youth cares little about nature's music, the beauties that awaken the eye or arouse the secret recesses of the body. It is a kind of mutant youth, devoid of all human desire, inhabited by and obsessed with a burning dream of purity and redemption. It is a youth reserved for the noble battle for the faith in which death is given and received with terrifying detachment. The lawful and the unlawful are the only two borders setting their horizons and marking their moral field: they sacrifice themselves to establish the one and they fight to the death to eradicate the other. A youth without any generosity, without guts, without reason, and without restraint, entirely stirred up by a devastating flood, the flood of dogma that commands one to suffer and cause suffering, to annihilate, and to die without the slightest feeling! Young people spying on each other in the street, ready to savagely pick a fight at the least suspicious gesture. Weapons speak with an ease and a frequency that make life laughable, a mere temporary accident squeezed between two probabilities in which the variable has become more unpredictable than ever.

In this land subjected to what they claim to be divine law, the law of discernment, justice, and compassion, men and women sneak around as if under a death sentence. When someone puts his hand in his pocket, under his coat or his gandoura, people hold their breath, hearts begin to pound wildly, legs tense up ready to start running madly. It is not uncommon for a gun or a dagger to flash forth—a feline leap, a gesture as swift as lightning. The result is a man, covered with knife cuts or riddled with bullets, who puts up a struggle in a pool of blood like an animal in a ritual sacrifice. There is no helping hand, no reaction of indignation. The passersby, overcome with panic, scatter and flee in every direction as if in a poultry yard over which a falcon hovers. The citizens have internalized terror, they have become mere beasts concerned with their own survival.

Since the preacher-lawmakers have seized power to make the reign of Equity a reality, to govern according to the law and the will of God, confidence reigns everywhere: the sovereign commander, according to divine decree, receives his divan gun in hand.

Books—the closeness of them, their contact, their smell, and their contents—constitute the safest refuge against this world of horror. They are the most pleasant and the most subtle means of traveling to a more compassionate planet. How will Boualem go on living now that they have separated him from his books, his most invigorating nourishment? He is like a plant that has been torn from the soil, separated from liquid and light, its two vital necessities. He has been excluded from the life of books. He has been exiled from all the landmarks of his childhood: values trampled, symbols corrupted, spaces disfigured and wrecked.

Today he would so much like to retrace again the tracks of that impoverished and marvelous childhood. But, undoubtedly, that will never come to be. His neighborhood, now even more overpopulated and deteriorated, has become a high-risk area. The religious militia has links with the underworld and with traffickers on all sides to engage in punitive actions against people who are hostile to the new order, against citizens they judge to be amoral, that is to say intellectuals, artists, and eccentrics. The stadium where, in his youthful vigor, he used to run after the soccer ball, is now the site of a gigantic mosque where the most malicious preachers take turns orating and where lists of men to be punished are regularly posted.

Boualem closes his eyes the better to see with his inward gaze those places so dear to his heart, places that today wear an unrecognizable face as a result of their disfigurements. Huddled inside himself, wrapped around his memories like a wood louse to keep them warm, he sends out this desperate prayer:

"My God, show me the way. For their path is not mine."

Does death make noise
as it moves?

In the courtyard's shriveled lemon tree, Boualem Yekker hears the woodpigeons coo. Blissful birds! They have not yet been forced to change their ways and songs, to temper melodies that would contradict the throbbing of their hearts. Birds are the very personification of liberty. As soon as some sky ceases to live up to the image of their desires, they gather together, confer, and take flight on a very long migration on which some of them lose their life. That is the price for living as one with your desires, in landscapes and horizons attuned to yourself. Birds don't submit, don't shiver pathetically in a climate that crushes them; they prefer to spread their wings and break through the horizon.

What skies will Boualem take off for in order to find rest and a humane community? Will it be possible for him to flee the heartless season that comes down on the land and find a climate that suits him? Is it still possible to meet a brother with a loving and poetic face on these precipitant roads where Dogma floats like a shrieking flag, and death lies nearby in ambush and ready to take out its spear, in the face of Madness crouching over the world like an immense cloud? Boualem would so much like to have a brother who, with the face of wisdom and liberty, would take him by the hand; together they would make their escape. But the world is a desert, insanity has transformed it into an ossuary. Spiritual enlightenment has arrived like a hurricane: in the territories that have been weeded out only insomniac watchmen remain, watchmen constantly scanning the devastated horizons to catch the rebellious soul.

Territories devoid of friendship, land devoid of intelligence, a desert without the refreshing stop of some intractable book that stirs the wound of questions and the seeds of insolence. The city has started to split into two antagonistic spaces: one, the majority, filled with men sparked by faith and certitude, and the other handed over to questioning, anxiety, and bullying. The two do not communicate, do not look at each other, do not greet each other. And one of the spaces has ended up reducing the other to silence before eradicating it. Today it prances around all by itself, rigged out in flamboyant certainties.

One day, people grew tired of thinking, weariness swooped down over their intelligence, and reason wavered. Those who were waiting—spiders weaving darkness, patient and persistent spiders who are made to stumble and relinquish by thinking—then came out and spread themselves far and wide. Like the irreversible nightfall.

It is in the night that people henceforth move forward, without a single illuminated reference point. Music and dance have been banned. Anything that kindles feelings of sacrilege in human beings has been banned. The young barely know how to sing; they are busy glorifying the dogma that excludes, peddling martyrdom and imposing it. Only dreaming is still allowed, to those who know how to find refuge within themselves. It is the only autonomous area that keeps the prison wardens at a distance.

And so, for lack of having a life, Boualem Yekker dreams. He replaces people with ghosts. He replaces the dwarfed history limping along in its little shoes with the grandiloquent myth that lifts the world's wings with a breath of poetry. But humanity has become bogged down in such ugliness that it will have a hard time finding the providential poet who can manage to adorn it and make it bearable.

Boualem Yekker is not that poet. He is only a humble dreamer who has not been visited by poetry. Of course, the desire to grasp the quintessence of the world and imprison it in writing has haunted him as it has haunted so many simple and disabled men who stealthily cross our streets, figures we do not even see. But Boualem did not live with the illusion for long; he quickly realized that others had created the books he could not create—and so admirably that they deter even the most presumptuous from attempting to compete. Boualem became instead a reader and a salesman of the jewels that his mind and hands had proven incapable of crafting. He did so without joy in his heart; suddenly accepting his own death, he understood that nothing of himself would remain beyond his disappearance. Boualem accepted dying.

Perhaps he will be a writer in another life? It is true that a single lifetime is too short to accomplish all that you want. There are so many deformities you would like to correct, so many events you would like to approach from another angle, so many trails you would like to cover over, so many wounds or affronts you would like to erase: at least one other life is needed to do this.

Still, it is frightening what you can experience in fifty years. Every time Boualem embarks on a retrospective of his life, something that occurs rather often these days, he conjures images and memories that seem to come from so far away, from a time immemorial. To reach him they snake in and out between endless summers, miles and miles of icy winds, valleys, rivers, and mountains. Beautiful and nostalgic music, music sad enough to make you weep, music from the magnificent and merciless time in which birth and death, separation and reunion are wedded. To stop each moment and exact its flesh from it, squeeze the last drop of sap from it. You feel like blocking every exit of the universe so that time will remain your prisoner, so that the whirlwind that pulls you to your death will be stopped.

Boualem has always been an early riser. Since he has been living alone he is even more so; long bouts of insomnia are no stranger to him and dawn often catches him with his eyes wide open. He has become his own constant guest—a strange feeling—and visits himself in great detail. He scrutinizes his past in every direction to identify hospitable shelters, benevolent lights, and invigorating stops. A kind of backwash rocks him between restful beaches, in a muted music like the rustling of palms. Sometimes an unexpected wind blows back a forgotten scent. A violent perfume that pierces him and then clings to him with fierce claws lacerating his skin. A kaleidoscope of the memory in which years, seasons, faces, and landscapes parade by in too great a rush, jostling and trampling each other. Some images linger more than others, deep scars, impregnable totems that time cannot overturn and bury. A buzzing, a groaning of memories bogged down in the hermetic room of the past, desperately banging on the door to get some fresh air. It happens that one of them escapes from this closed and obdurate world to take shape in the present. It conquers the magic spell of time and breaks out, a blessed convict who cancels his sentence and once again finds the exultation of the blood pulsing in freedom. He materializes in front of us, a messenger of life and death, a dark spark epitomizing the omnipotence of nothingness.

Boualem is sitting on a public bench at high elevation overlooking the superb harbor vista of the city in which he was born, a city that tumbles down like a herd of goats from a curtain of hills and then scatters around the shore. In the evening, its lights draw the illusion of a starry sky reflected in the water—a milky way stretching, sometimes curving, or simpy closing in on itself.

But the perspective before Boualem's eyes is a daytime view in which the whiteness of the blocks of houses, the bouquets of greenery, and a dazzling light add an ornamental touch to the beauty of the bay. A strange peace floats over the city that, after all, is bleeding so dreadfully inside, this city predisposed to joy but from which joy has been banned. Boualem watches with the gaze of someone who is leaving a place never to return. Or the gaze of someone who is observing the place where he is going to die. Which amounts to the same thing. It is terrible to be watching spaces in which you have been moving around for forty years; it almost makes your life unreal. Only these spaces possess a reality that survives by expunging every human existence that may have stopped or settled there.

To go through life as you swim through a current: the water foams and roils unendingly, forbidding any face to become fixed, any memory to linger. You reach the other shore completely destitute, a memory in pain the only relic of your crossing.

Boualem activates this memory, tinkers with it until he has made it into a quivering wound. He would like to extract some images from it, rekindle a few sparks in it by which to warm himself. Together with his memory, he also interrogates the city about the traces of the child and the adolescent he once was. He stops at street corners, in front of stores, indistinct areas for gathering clues, awakening smells, dusting off buried faces. But the flesh is lacking in these evocations, agitation and palpitation are lacking. Emotions felt for the first time and the magic of discovery have vanished forever. Innumerable weaknesses have come between him and the images he searches for. When he does miraculously succeed in resuscitating them, they prove to be dull and lackluster, dead wood he gathers up on memory's shores and vainly blows on in the hope of injecting it with some spark of life. By sheer insistence, a few twigs sometimes light up with a feeble, convulsive motion, like a small animal hanging on to life with a few jolts before breathing its last. Then all becomes motionless again, the flat calm of time that kills in silence and without any passion whatsoever.

Still, they were happy. Boualem remembers a family doing its utmost to create a minimum of tenderness in an occupied country living in misery and humiliation. Everything had a value to the scale of its scarcity: bread, shirts mended over and over again, shoes, books read and reread. The big brother whom Boualem loved deeply was a worry to the family because he was so small. When he was twenty, Boualem, who was twelve, trembled to see his older brother congeal into so unassuming a height. He would spend his time trying to find out at what age growth ceases, always dreaming that his brother would encounter a miracle that would stretch him out considerably before he stopped growing. Lately, Boualem has been thinking about him a great deal, regretting that adult life has offered them so few opportunities to see each other. But is that not an egotistic thought? It is probably only his own childhood the bookseller would search for through this early witness.

Boualem dreams of walking in a deserted and silent street, shaded by chestnut trees. But the city is overpopulated, it is swarming like an ant heap no matter what the time of day, no matter what the season. Berbers have multiplied like flies, sometimes making you think of spontaneous generation. Sidewalks barely hold the crowds that spill out into the streets, blocking traffic and drowning it in their tide. This city, once beautiful and voluptuous in the amber aromas of the evening, has become unlivable. The birds that used to haunt the trees, orchestrating dusky celebrations, have emigrated to more inhabitable skies. If Boualem, too, were forced to leave, it would almost be without regret; for this land is "chasing its children away," as one of the local proverbs says.

In the first months, when he would see the bearded militia parade through the large arteries, he was struck by the disparity between these medieval warriors and this sensual and cheerful city baring its chest to the sea. He used to tell himself that the city would not be long in expelling the parasitic body that was such an insult to the landscape. Thus he waited for things to return to normal, for the messengers of fanaticism to go back to their dark corners, and for the city, open to the sea breezes, to go back to its sumptuous stretching exercises. How many men like him turned out to be wrong! It was enough for beauty and reason to doze off for a moment, abandoning their defenses, for night to shove day out and pour across the city like a horrifying flood. Now it is no longer possible to go back; every dike and every lock has been broken. Uncontrollable hysteria has overtaken the city, demolishing the barriers. All fanatic energy is stretched like an archer's bow, turned toward a dream of society's purification. Exorcism by blood and total deluge.

Boualem would like to take public transportation as in the past, to feel the human warmth fueled by physical proximity and indelicate chatter. But this city is no longer his. This new race of the devout, who know nothing about music and concerts and the fellowship of a shared glass, this recruited youth that disdains the flights of the heart and the beauty of the dream has banished him from this space where he has walked, dreamed, loved, where he has rejoiced and rebelled. His city with its bewitching iridescence, his adventurous city stretching its hands toward the open sea and panting beneath the waves like a young girl's breast, his city has been transformed into a desert and a leper hospital!

From his park bench, he watches it as it winds its way toward the sea as if looking for a way to flee, as it decays under a sky whose light does not illuminate but burns. The streets come down in a gentle slope, escorted by trees. Boualem has gazed at these landscapes so many times that his eyes have lost their watchfulness: subjected to a force of diversion, they often wander off, look without seeing, busy with something else while the panorama offers itself to him, not real but a simple mirror in which dreams and memories frolic.

Before, these scenes had brought him not only pleasure and comfort but also a deep melancholy awakened by the shadow of death. The adornments with which the seasons sprinkled the brimming body of the city would make him think above all of time passing, of death seated at the end of the road. He'd catch himself wondering: does death make any noise as it advances?

Yes, this city that contents itself with the beauties nature has bestowed on it, that has not—like other cities—tamed rivers, spanned hills, constructed impressive buildings, this pampered and tormented city has often made him think of orgasm and death, of orgasm in death.

Childhood returns like an ebb tide, submerges him, delivers him, hands and feet tied, to the tortures of memory.

Caressing time the wrong way. Walking with a

limp over your own tracks. What scenes of destruc-
tion you pace through, but also what lifeblood and
what suddenly awakened dreams crackle beneath
our footsteps like husks that have held their fruit too
long!

A stubborn child pursues you, a child forever
hurt who blames you—wordlessly—for having abandoned him in the mazes of time, a deadly spider web
whose prisoner he remains. The child holds his
hands out to you, begging for your indulgence. For
he doesn't understand your helplessness. He doesn't
understand that you, too, are a prisoner at the other
end of the time that carries you relentlessly toward
ugliness and annihilation. The child and you are
under the constraint of a harrowing divorce, of an
inevitable separation.

But sometimes, when miracle and magic link up,
the child and you are joined again. For example, in
the wondrous adventure that makes you a father. A
human being detaches itself from you to lead its own
life. Spectator of yourself, you again see and relive
your hesitations, your discoveries, your wonderment,
and your disappointments. Being double, suddenly
extended in time, you grow familiar with splitting
and omnipresence. A burgeoning, blooming life,

often getting hurt as well. A miraculous life that pulses to the rhythm of dazzling seasons.

Boualem has followed funeral processions, too. In countless numbers. Time again. That following removes its share of life, swoops down like a bird of prey on joy and beauty and tears them to shreds, its talons leaving immense holes that no amount of courage or oblivion manages to patch. We are this crumbling body that, day after day and year after year, leaves bits of itself behind on every obstacle, is stripped bare, and atrophies until it presents itself fleshless and impotent, almost mummified, to the devastating force, the heavy truncheon of time that finishes it off, to the dizzying fall into the night, into the absolute of nothingness.

Boualem Yekker does not possess the certainties of the crowds around him. Today he could have been more tranquil. The price to be paid is not an exorbitant one: it would have been enough to join the herd, to bleat in unison, to watch out for false notes. Besides, the faithful are there to make the task easier: their pious clamors stifle any question. It would have been enough to grab a pair of those blinders they so generously offer and sport them. He would have been immersed in the peace that blindness secures. It would have been enough to take the gentle slope of abdication, of the abjuration of exercising his intelligence. With just a little effort, Boualem would have won the peace down here and—who knows?—perhaps the peace of the hereafter. The warmth of the herd brings security, shows the lines of evidence, protects you against the icy stings of doubt. It marks the course; it gives the illusion of the straight path, the path leading from a noisy and coarse gathering toward the paradise of the narrow-minded. The sheep that moves away from the herd immediately contracts mange. It is met with rebuffs, the imagery of suffering, the cursing rhetoric that dogma enlists to punish intelligence and divert its queries.

Sad references today. Devotion as the standard for grandeur. Faith: a desert of stones; a gravel wasteland with a scraped face. Boualem Yekker is a man lost between this desert of faith and the paradise of books. Books, his old companions, the saving grace of dreaming and intelligence brought together!

By now they have no doubt burned all his books in an exorcizing fire. They understand the danger in words, all the words they cannot manage to domesticate and anesthetize. For words, put end to end, bring doubt and change. Words above all must not conceive of the utopia of another form of truth, of unsuspected paths, of another place of thought. You do not easily part with utopia; it is an acid that cuts holes in the opacity of dogma, holes where controversy lies and where questions proliferate. Those who, in defiance of the command, clutch uncontrolled words must be banished from a state in which they can do harm. By gagging, the so necessary liquidation. For from now on, the world belongs to the therapists of the spirit; the city resounds with their sermons and their rhythmic steps.

The city with the many forms of iridescence that once danced on the foam, an adolescent swathed in a dress of azure blue and sun, is now a field of merciless thorns. Beauty is a decapitated flower. Love is a recumbent effigy, a dead tree. Song flees into exile.

On the sea, ablaze with the setting sun, a babbling runs across the water, awakening golden brown reptiles on its surface. The solemnity of dusk. The world marks a stopping point, gravely contemplates the sun's funeral. The air has mellowed, laden with tenderness and a sadness that tightens your throat. A moment of rapture and nostalgia in which unforgettable images and feelings—the very rhythm of time and of universal forgiveness— return. Each object seems to give up the sweetest and most conciliatory thing it conceals in order to make the night, which soon will erase and shroud everything, more bearable. All around Boualem, birds begin their dusky utterances and their squabbles. They raise a noisy protest against this decree, repeated every evening, that soon will gag them. A very long time ago, as night unfurled across the city, one of Boualem's favorite games had been guessing the exact site of a particular building, institution, or public park.

The sweet sadness bequeathed by every day that leaves us behind has not yet been chased out of this country. But the course of time has gone crazy, and who dares swear to the appearance of the following day.

Will there be another spring?